FINTAN'S FIFTEEN

ALAN
NOLAN

D0412712

YOU'LL LAUGH, YOU'LL CRY
...YOU'LL HURL.

THE O'BRIEN PRESS
DUBLIN

For Dad.

First published 2014 by The O'Brien Press Limited
12 Terenure Road East, Rathgar, Dublin 6, Ireland

Tel: +353 1 492 3333; Fax: +353 1 492 2777
Email: books@obrien.ie
Website: www.obrien.ie

ISBN: 978-1-84717-253-2

8 7 6 5 4 3 2 1
18 17 16 15 14

Editing: The O'Brien Press Limited
Printing: Nørhaven, Denmark
The paper used in this book is produced using pulp from managed forests

The O'Brien Press receives assistance from

IN THE DUST OF DEFEAT AS WELL AS IN THE LAUREL OF VICTORY, THERE IS GLORY TO BE FOUND.

JJ MEAGHER

Okay. Here's the story. *Sin é an sceal*, as they say.

My name is Rusty and I am proud to say I am a Ballybreen Terrier.

If you had asked me was I a proud Terrier three months ago, the answer would have been very different.

You see, only three months ago the Ballybreen Terriers were the worst Under 12s hurling team in the county. In fact we were the worst in the country. To be honest, we were the worst in the entire world. If they played hurling in outer space (and I've no reason to believe that they don't – imagine the *poc fadas* you could have in zero gravity!) I'm sure the Mars U12s could have beaten us with one tentacle tied behind their backs.

5

Plain and simple: we were ROTTEN, we were WOEFUL, we were WUBBISH. Sorry, RUBBISH.

So how did such an unbelievably crummy team end up winning the Lonergan Cup?

Well, it wasn't easy. It's a long story of hard work, loads of training, LOADS of fun, new friends, old friends… and one young fella who had quite a bit of experience in fighting against almost impossible odds. (That's not me, by the way.)

But I'm getting ahead of myself.

Maybe a proper introduction is in order. I'm Rusty, but I don't mean I'm covered in dirty, red, metal flakes. Rusty is my nickname. My real name is Raymond Arantes. I'm from Brazil, originally, my whole family are, and we've lived in Ballybreen for six years.

I only took up GAA last year, though. And despite being in the worst team in Ireland, yadda, yadda (see above) I LOVE HURLING!

When I first picked up a hurley stick, I realised what I wanted to do with my life. The hurley just fitted so well in my hand, it felt like an extension of my own arm. It felt like a part of me that

I didn't even realise was missing. At that moment, it was like the clouds parted and the sun shone down on my head and my head alone – I think I heard music, but it could have been one of the mums at the side of the field playing her car radio too loud.

I knew then – I wanted to be a hurler, I wanted to play for my county, I wanted to win an All-Ireland medal!

But first, I had to join a team.

Ballybreen is not a big town, but it's a young town. Plenty of young families moved here during the boom, ourselves included. There's only one club, and really only one age group that has enough players to make up a panel – the under 12s.

Luckily for me, that's my age.

There aren't many upsides to being eleven, but the long summer holiday is one of them. In the last couple of weeks of school before the break we were learning all about the legend of Cú Chulainn. You know, the one where he was called Setanta to start with and then, because he was attacked by this guy Culann's massive hound, and accidentally-on-purpose, totally in self defence, dispatched the crackers canine off to doggy heaven, had to take on the role of the dog and become 'the hound of Culann'. He had a dog's life, basically. Well, it was the way he massacred the mental mongrel that caught my attention: he used a hurl and sliotar. Our teacher told us that on that very day Setanta (Cú to his pals) invented the sport of hurling! That sounded so cool, I was instantly hooked!

Our school wasn't a big, sporty school, but Ballybreen had a very small GAA club, so I went around and signed up.

I'll never forget the look on the bainisteoir's face when I walked in to the big, rusty, metal container that served as the Ballybreen clubhouse, equipment room, dressing room and storage facility for dead flies and mice droppings: the look was pretty much disbelief with a large side order of 'this young fella can't be serious and/or all-in-it.' New sign-ups were so few and far between that he had to search the whole dingy clubhouse for a pen to take down my details, and when he eventually found one it wouldn't work.

That was Mr Massey. That was seven bainisteoirs ago. Yup, in the last eighteen months the Ballybreen Terriers U12s hurling team has had eight managers. It was Pat Massey when I started, followed by Billy 'The Bull' Robinson, then Gerry Lynham (I liked him), then 'Hacker' Whelan (he never told us his first name), Tadhg 'Ol' One Eye' O'Sullivan, followed by 'Nervous' Naoise O'Neill, then 'Clueless' Colm Faulkner, finally by the latest and definitely-not-the-greatest Frank 'Fidgety' Furlong.

Players have come and gone as well, but Paddy Fox and Jerome 'Halfpint' O'Reilly have been here as long as I have. I call Paddy 'iPaddy' because I've never seen him without his headphones on. He's always listening to music and can never hear what you're saying. A bit of a drawback when you're playing a match.

The other person who's been here as long as I have, even longer, is Katie Bell, AKA 'Dinger' Bell. She's the team's number one fan and cheers loudest at all the matches. In fact, she's usually the only one cheering at our matches. She's twirly-baton-style majorette for the Ballybreen Spinners and is clever and has a great smile and lovely brown hair and smells nice. Well, you get the idea.

Oh. And then there's Ollie the Dog. Ollie is the Ballybreen Terriers' mascot. He's medium-sized, tan-coloured and eats a lot. I don't know what kind of dog he is, but if I had to guess I'd say he's a cross between an Irish terrier and a three-toed sloth. I've never met such a lazy dog, or such a fat one. He sleeps in a plywood kennel beside the clubhouse, and once he didn't come out for three days because he couldn't fit through the door.

Katie has him on a fitness regime now – low-fat dogfood, semi-regular walks and no, repeat NO biscuits (Kimberley are his favourite). We all love Ollie, but Fidgety Furlong hated him. Furlong disliked anyone or anything that wasn't lean, mean and ready for action. Which meant he wasn't overly fond of the Ballybreen Terriers either.

I'll never forget Fidgety Furlong's last match as bainisteoir.

It was a wild, wet and windy afternoon. As a team the Terriers had our ups and downs. Well, we'd mainly just had downs. And this was definitely one of them. We'd just lost a home game to our old rivals the Kilmore Killers, 0-0 to 2-17. It wasn't the first time we'd lost to them, not by a long chalk. They'd beaten us three times in the last six months. In fact, we hadn't won a match against the Kilmore Killers, or anyone else for that matter, for as long as anyone could remember. Seventeen straight losses in a row.

Even Katie looked a little deflated as we left the field.

'Well done,' she said as she clapped our backs coming off the pitch. 'You all gave it your best shot.'

'Their best shot?' said Fidgety Furlong, walking behind me. 'Their best shot?! They SHOULD be shot!'

His face was turning an interesting shade of crimson as the rain poured down it, plastering what little hair he has to his large forehead and dripping off his long, beak-like nose.

'You gave that game away, lads,' he snarled. 'You never even put up a fight!'

He spoke too soon. As we opened the rickety doors to our crumbling clubhouse, we were greeted by the sight of our keeper, Iggy McKenna, lying on the floor being completely marmelised by our left winger, Seamus Muldoon. 'You eejit!' Seamus was shouting. 'Save a goal? You couldn't save your communion money!'

Halfpint and iPaddy were trying to separate them as the two lads rolled around, upsetting the snacks table and knocking over team photos. Fidgety Furlong was furious (not a pretty sight) and waded in, trying to pull them apart with one arm, while wiping snots from his enormous nose with the sleeve of his other. 'Seamus! Iggy! Break it up now or you won't get a game at all next week!'

'Don't care,' said Seamus, 'I won't be here next week – I quit!'

'Me too!' said Iggy, getting up off the floor and grabbing his kit. He and Seamus marched out of the clubhouse into the torrential downpour, slamming the door behind them. There was a peal of thunder. The weather really was turning nasty. So was Fidgety Furlong.

'Actually,' he said, 'me too. I've been meaning to say this for a few weeks, but I've been offered a job in Australia.' He glared at us. 'And after the shambles of the last few matches, I've decided to take it. This afternoon's pitiful performance was the last straw,' he said, 'I fly out on Thursday.'

'I'd like to say I'll miss you all, but I wouldn't want to lie,' he added. 'To be honest, I'll be delighted to see the back of each and every one of you, you lazy pack of –' (A loud peal of thunder drowned out his last word. Probably just as well.) 'And before I go, I'd just like you to know that the Ballybreen Terriers are the worst, most disorganised, most untalented team that I've ever had the displeasure to manage.'

And Fidgety came to us from St. Gobnet's, so he knew what he was talking about.

'Good luck getting yourselves a manager,' he said sarcastically. 'From now on you'll be someone else's problem.'

He pointed at us with a bony finger, the recently wiped snots glistening on his wet sleeve. 'If you've any sense at all, you'll do like Iggy and Seamus did – give up.' And with that he blew his long nose on a filthy handerchief and stalked out into the rain.

A few of the remaining players looked at each other, then quickly gathered up their stuff and left too.

Katie looked stunned. There was another roar of thunder and Ollie put his paws over his ears. There was only him, Katie, Halfpint, iPaddy, me and a handful of the younger ones left in the clubhouse. The last of the Ballybreen Terriers.

'So,' said Katie, 'what do we do now?'

iPaddy took off his headphones and looked around. 'Huh? What happened? Where did everybody go?' he asked. 'Did I miss something?'

After iPaddy's mum had collected him and Halfpint, Katie and I sat down to review the Terriers' situation. It was pretty dire. 'Remember how hard it was to get even somebody like Fidgety Furlong to manage us?' I asked Katie. 'Everyone else turned us down. Who will be bainisteoir now?'

'You've bigger problems than that,' Katie replied. 'You haven't got a team to manage. There's only you, iPaddy and Halfpint left!'

She was right. But there comes a point when you go so low that you really can't go any further down. All you can do is get climbing back up.

Sure, the Ballybreen Terriers had no talent, no discipline and, more importantly, no players. But they were still MY team. We still had me and iPaddy and Halfpint, and we still had our number one (and only) fan, Katie. As long as I could hold a hurl, I'd keep on fighting – just like Cú Chulainn.

Ollie whimpered. *Don't worry, boy,* I thought, *I promise I won't fight you!*

Okay, if we were going to rebuild the Terriers, we'd better start by tidying up the clubhouse. It was a mess after the fight. Actually, it was usually a mess; the casual observer wouldn't have noticed the difference.

Katie started to hang up the photos that Iggy and Seamus had knocked down while I put empty juice cartons into a black plastic sack. Ollie helpfully helped himself to the remains of a packet of cheese and onion crisps.

When the clubhouse looked a little bit better, Katie opened a bottle of lemonade.

'Make mine a rock shandy,' I said. 'I need the hard stuff right now.'

I sat, thinking. 'What the Terriers need,' I said to Katie after a while, 'is an injection of fresh blood. New players. A brand new bainisteoir.'

'Hmmm,' said Katie. She was staring up at one of the photos she had rescued from under the changing bench. 'You know, the Terriers weren't always this bad. A couple of years ago, before you joined, we were actually pretty good. We had the players, we had the potential. We could have won the cup.'

'And it was all down to one guy.' She held up the photo she had plucked from the rusty wall so I could see. It showed a smiling, ginger-haired kid of about ten years of age with a face full of freckles and a determined look in his eyes. He was dressed in Terriers colours and held a broken hurley stick across his broad (and, it has to be said) chunky chest.

'Fintan Lonergan,' said Katie. 'This was taken on the day he smashed his hurl against the Castlewilde Wolfhounds' goalpost. He scored a goal too! 3-18 to 1-9 in that game. All thanks to Fintan. Our best goal scorer ever, a powerful, straight shot every time.

A great hurler for his age, from a great hurling family – his own granddad donated the Lonergan Cup!'

'And we could have taken the cup that year, the Terriers were going great.'

Ollie padded over to where Katie was sitting and snuggled in to her, resting his sizeable head in her lap.

'But then, one day, he just stopped coming to training. No explanation. He wouldn't answer his mobile and wouldn't come to the phone when we called his house. His mum said he had retired. Retired! At ten years old! She said he'd given up hurling for good, and that was that.'

'Ah, come on,' I said. 'Nobody gives up hurling for good.'

'Well, that's what they said,' said Katie. 'He sounded like he'd made up his mind.'

'Well, if he won't play any more, maybe ... he'd coach?' My mind was racing. 'We need a bainisteoir as well as players. Maybe this Fintan guy could help us out!'

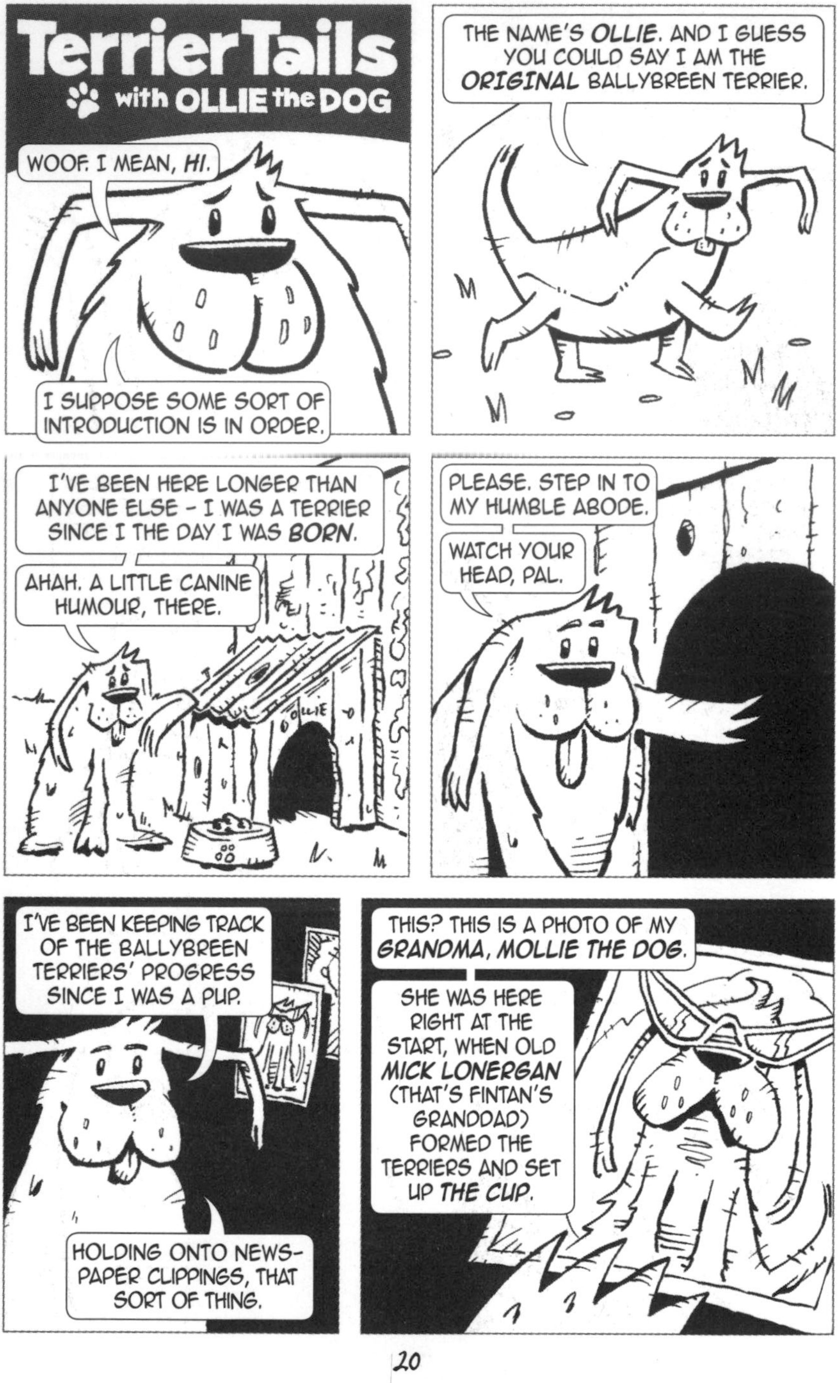
Terrier Tails
with OLLIE the DOG
WOOF. I MEAN, HI.
I SUPPOSE SOME SORT OF INTRODUCTION IS IN ORDER.
THE NAME'S OLLIE. AND I GUESS YOU COULD SAY I AM THE ORIGINAL BALLYBREEN TERRIER.
I'VE BEEN HERE LONGER THAN ANYONE ELSE - I WAS A TERRIER SINCE I THE DAY I WAS BORN.
AHAH. A LITTLE CANINE HUMOUR, THERE.
OLLIE
PLEASE. STEP IN TO MY HUMBLE ABODE.
WATCH YOUR HEAD, PAL.
I'VE BEEN KEEPING TRACK OF THE BALLYBREEN TERRIERS' PROGRESS SINCE I WAS A PUP.
HOLDING ONTO NEWS-PAPER CLIPPINGS, THAT SORT OF THING.
THIS? THIS IS A PHOTO OF MY GRANDMA, MOLLIE THE DOG.
SHE WAS HERE RIGHT AT THE START, WHEN OLD MICK LONERGAN (THAT'S FINTAN'S GRANDDAD) FORMED THE TERRIERS AND SET UP THE CUP.

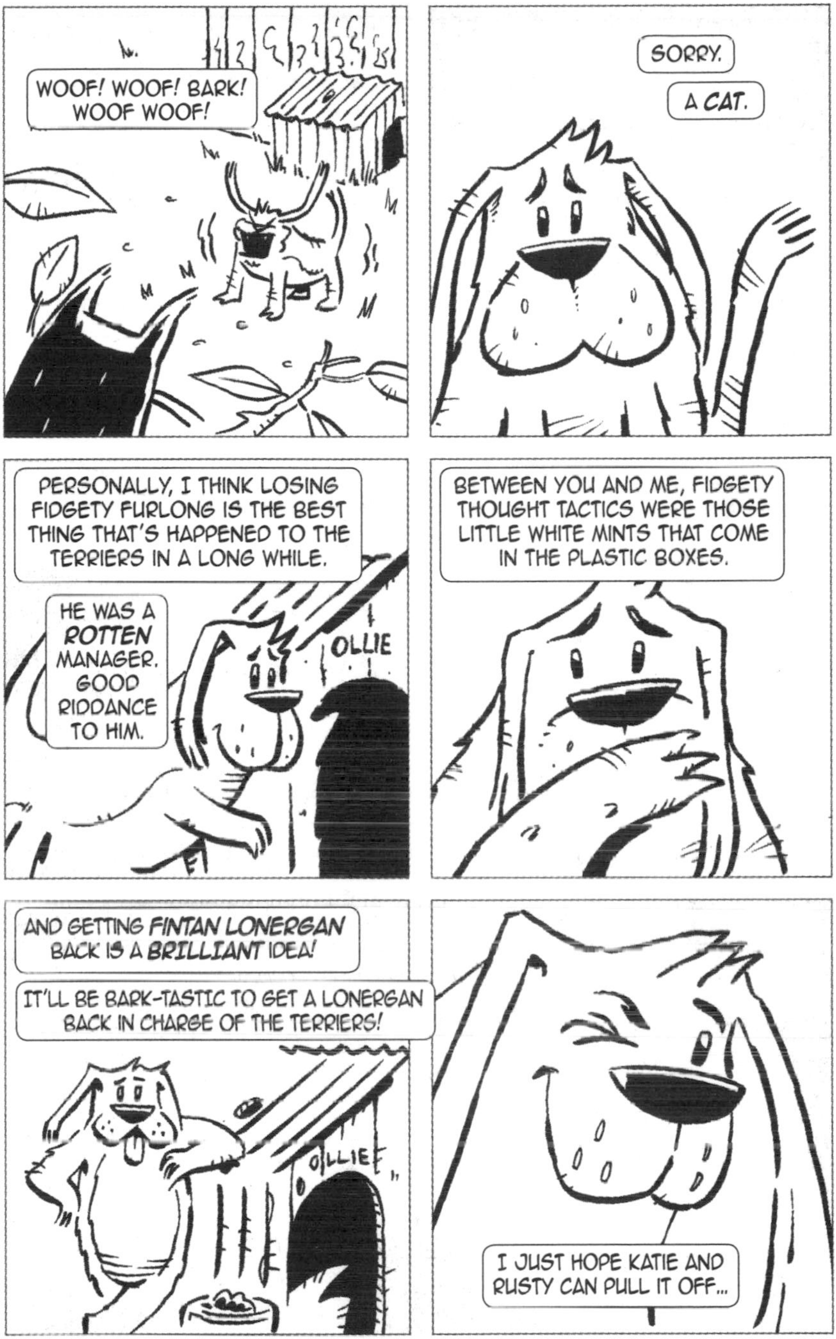

WOOF! WOOF! BARK! WOOF WOOF!
SORRY.
A CAT.
PERSONALLY, I THINK LOSING FIDGETY FURLONG IS THE BEST THING THAT'S HAPPENED TO THE TERRIERS IN A LONG WHILE.
HE WAS A ROTTEN MANAGER. GOOD RIDDANCE TO HIM.
OLLIE
BETWEEN YOU AND ME, FIDGETY THOUGHT TACTICS WERE THOSE LITTLE WHITE MINTS THAT COME IN THE PLASTIC BOXES.
AND GETTING FINTAN LONERGAN BACK IS A BRILLIANT IDEA!
IT'LL BE BARK-TASTIC TO GET A LONERGAN BACK IN CHARGE OF THE TERRIERS!
OLLIE
I JUST HOPE KATIE AND RUSTY CAN PULL IT OFF...

IT LOOKS LIKE THERE'S A BIT OF A SCHEMOZZLE IN THE PARALLELOGRAM.
MÍCHEÁL O'HEHIR

The next day I met Katie at the clubhouse, where she was feeding Ollie. 'Low fat dogfood again, Ollie,' she was saying as she poured some dry food pellets into Ollie's red bowl. Ollie snuffled around the pellets and glanced up at Katie. He didn't look impressed.

'Right. So, what's the plan?' I said as I leaned my bike against the clubhouse wall. 'Well, I suppose, we just cycle over to his house and ask him,' said Katie. 'Fair enough,' I said, and we both hopped on our bikes and headed off, with Ollie running behind us. Well, I say 'running'; 'waddling' would be a more accurate word. We had to stop several times on the journey to allow him to catch up with us.

The storm from the day before had passed and the sun was shining as we cycled out of town towards where Fintan lived. Katie's bike was pretty new. I think she must have gotten it for her birthday, but mine was old and lived up to my name – it was a bit rusty.

Boy, it was hot! 'How… much … further …?' I panted. Katie moved up to third gear. 'Not far now. The next left. It's the house at the end of the laneway.'

We turned into a private road that wasn't tarmaced and had a line of grass and weeds growing down the middle. It was bordered on both sides by thick hedges. At the end of the lane was a gate made out of an old green front door on its side. Some post was sticking out of its sideways letterbox and Katie plucked it out as we laid our bikes against the overgrown hedge. Ollie finally arrived and collapsed in a heap in front of the gate.

'The bikes will be fine here with Ollie, it's quiet enough,' said Katie.

'You can say that again,' I replied. The laneway looked deserted, as if nobody had been down it in years.

We walked towards the house. 'You know,' said Katie, 'I remember one match that Fintan played. We were up against the Lismartin Hackers and Fintan was up close to the Lismartin goal. All of a sudden he spotted a break down at the far end beside the Terriers' goal and he ran full tilt up the length of the pitch. I've never seen anyone run so fast. Just as the Lismartin striker hit the ball Fintan launched himself in front of the shot and blocked it with his chest. He was black and blue afterwards, but he said it was worth it. Or that other time he did this crazy jump, a kind of somersault, right over the heads of two Rathmore defenders – up an' over 'em! They were left scratching their heads, looking around, wondering where he had gone. He was behind them scoring a point! He called it his "Fionn MacCumhaill" leap.'

Fionn MacCumhaill, huh? I thought, *I love those Irish legends…*

Our feet crunched on the gravel pathway as we walked towards the house. I was a little nervous, I was about to meet the legend himself.

I looked up at the Lonergan family home. Despite the state of the laneway and the garden gate, the house looked clean and newly whitewashed, with six smallish windows at the front. A ginger cat looked at us curiously from around the corner of the building.

From somewhere behind us I could hear Ollie growl.

Katie winked at me and rang the doorbell. Deep inside the house we could hear the chime. It sounded like that old song, 'La Bamba'. For a long time there was no answer. Katie had raised her hand to press the doorbell again when the door was flung open to reveal a large red-headed woman with a towel on her head and the biggest teeth I'd ever seen. I took a step back, but when this woman spoke she had a lovely, sweet voice.

'Hello, my loves,' she said. 'Sorry, I was washing my hair. Are you selling lines for the sponsored walk?'

'No, Mrs Lonergan—' started Katie, but the large lady cut in. 'Oh! You're one of the Bells, aren't you? Katie, isn't it? I remember you. How's your mum? You must be here about the Spinners! Fundraising, is it? I'll get my purse.'

'No, Mrs Lonergan, it's not about the Spinners, it's about the Ballybreen Terriers. We're here to see Fintan.'

'Oh,' said Mrs Lonergan, 'the Terriers.' She looked at my red, mud-stained Terriers jersey (I rarely wear anything else) and then regarded Katie. 'Please, Mrs Lonergan, it's very important.'

'Is that post for me?' asked Mrs Lonergan. Katie looked down at the letters she had taken from the sideways letterbox. She had forgotten all about them. 'Post? Oh! Yes!' She handed the letters over.

'Thanks for saving me the trip to the postbox, my love,' said Mrs Lonergan. 'I have to warn you, you may have been better off saving yourselves a trip as well. Fintan mightn't want to see anyone today. He can be a little … moody, you know.'

Mrs Lonergan led us through the house, which was dark, quiet and empty. There was no sign of Fintan. Something else was missing too. 'Did you notice,' I whispered to Katie, 'no hurling photos, no medals, no trophies? I thought Fintan's family were hurling fanatics.' Katie raised her eyebrows and put her finger to her lips.

'This way, my loves,' said Mrs Lonergan as she stepped out the back door into a large yard surrounded by whitewashed cement block sheds with corrugated metal roofs and old-fashioned half doors. One of the sheds, the furthest from the door, was painted red and had large plywood boards covering the windows, which must have blocked out the light inside.

'Fintan's in there,' said Mrs Lonergan, pointing at the red shed, 'I'd knock first, my loves, if I were you.' She retreated into the kitchen and after a moment we could hear what sounded like a hairdryer.

Katie and I looked at each other and walked towards the red shed door, which, to our surprise, flew open suddenly.

In the doorway stood a boy of about twelve, who looked only vaguely like the photo of Fintan that Katie had shown me in the clubhouse.

This lad had greasy red hair, all sticking up on one side as if he had slept on it badly. In fact, he kind of looked greasy all over. He was overweight, wore thick-rimmed glasses, his red tee shirt was filthy and he was carrying a family-size bucket of southern fried chicken. He had a chicken leg in one hand and breadcrumbs around his lips. He looked as if he had just woken up.

Katie stepped forward. 'Eh … Fintan?'

'Fintan's not here today. Please call again.' He slammed the door.

The look of shock on Katie's face was priceless. She shouted
to the closed door. 'Fintan! It's me, Katie Bell! "Dinger" Bell?'
But we were answered with silence. Katie looked at me, her mouth
open in shock.

We had turned to walk away when we heard the slow creak of
a door opening. Fintan was standing in the doorway again, but this
time the chicken bucket was gone. He looked like he had made some
attempt at smoothing down his ginger hair, but he still had southern
fried breadcrumbs on his face. He was blinking in the sunlight.

'Katie…?'

He gestured for us to come in with the chicken leg he was
holding. He noticed it was still in his hand and chucked it into the
yard.

'Here, em, Tiddles,' he called. 'The, uh, cat loves chicken.' As
if from nowhere, Ollie appeared in the yard and started munching
on the chicken leg. 'Ollie …' Fintan whispered, almost to himself,
and shoved his glasses up on his nose with his thumb. He suddenly
brightened up. 'Come in! Welcome to my den!'

We went inside the red shed and, as I suspected, it was pretty
dark. And surprisingly roomy. The walls were covered with what

looked like dark red curtains, and against one wall was an old, faded, floral pattern sofa with torn cushions and springs emerging from its innards. There was a large depression on one side of the sofa. It looked Fintan-shaped. In front of the sofa was a flat screen TV with a DVD player and several different types of game consoles hooked up to it.

There were wires, cables and multi-coloured controllers everywhere, and the floor was littered with silver discs, empty games boxes and discarded fast food packaging. Ollie, having finished the chicken leg, came in and stuck his head in the southern fried chicken bucket that was lying on its side by the sofa.

'I'm sorry,' said Fintan, 'it's, uh, the maid's day off.'

'Fintan,' said Katie, 'this is Rusty.'

'Ray "Rusty" Arantes,' I said. 'Nice to, em, meet you!'

'What do you want, Dinger?' said Fintan. 'I'm very busy.' He took off his spectacles and put them back on again. 'I just need them for computer gaming.'

'They, um, suit you,' said Katie, glancing around at the scene of destruction. 'Well … Fintan, you see …'

Katie was hesitant and gave me a sideways glance. I stepped in. 'The Terriers are finished. Fidgety Furlong is gone. Most of the panel have quit. Look, Fintan, Katie and me need help. We need YOUR help.'

'Fidgety Furlong … hah,' Fintan snorted. 'What makes you think I want to help? What makes you think I give two hoots about the Ballybreen Terriers?'

He slumped down into the Fintan-shaped indentation in the sofa and picked up a games controller, his head down. The TV made 'ping' noises and there was the sound of simulated cheers.

Katie pursed her lips and a determined look came into her eyes. I knew that look. 'Fintan, your family set up the Ballybreen Terriers AND they set up the Lonergan Cup competition. The Lonergans even donated the cup we all play for.'

'Battered old scrap metal, found in the attic. Worthless,' said Fintan, his head still down and his eyes on the screen.

Katie stood in front of Fintan, blocking his view. 'No. It's not worthless. It's got your name on it. All we're asking for is your help. YOUR help, to help YOUR team, take back YOUR cup. Or at least to give it a go.' Fintan was craning his neck, trying to see past Katie, his fingers flying on the controller. The TV cheered as he scored a goal on-screen.

'Don't you want to hear those cheers for real?' asked Katie.

Fintan paused the game. 'I'm tired,' he said. 'Time for a nap.' To our surprise, he lay down on the sofa and turned his back on us. 'Fintan? Fintan!' said Katie, then looked at me. I shrugged. Fintan didn't move, he looked as if he was asleep. I'd never met a boy like him. He was so ... odd. We left in silence, closing the door behind us.

'He'll come around,' said Katie when we were back in the sunlit yard. 'I wouldn't bet on it,' I said, thinking that Mrs Lonergan may have been right about saving ourselves a trip. It certainly seemed like a wasted journey. We headed for the kitchen door.

Suddenly the door of the red shed slammed open again, and into the yard came Fintan. He looked somehow taller as he held a camán. Ollie came out of the shed, padded up beside him and sat at his feet. Fintan took off his glasses and laid them aside. Wordlessly, he tossed a sliotar into the air and hit it with a mighty blow. The crack of ash meeting leather resounded around the yard, the noise bouncing off the cement sheds, as the ball rocketed into the blue sky, way over the roof of Fintan's house. A flock of birds scattered as the sliotar flew by them. It just seemed to keep going up and up. We didn't hear it fall.

Ollie danced around Fintan's legs, yapping delightedly, and Katie rushed over to hug both of them. 'I'll do it,' said Fintan. Katie and I were so thrilled that we didn't stop to think about what might have changed his mind.

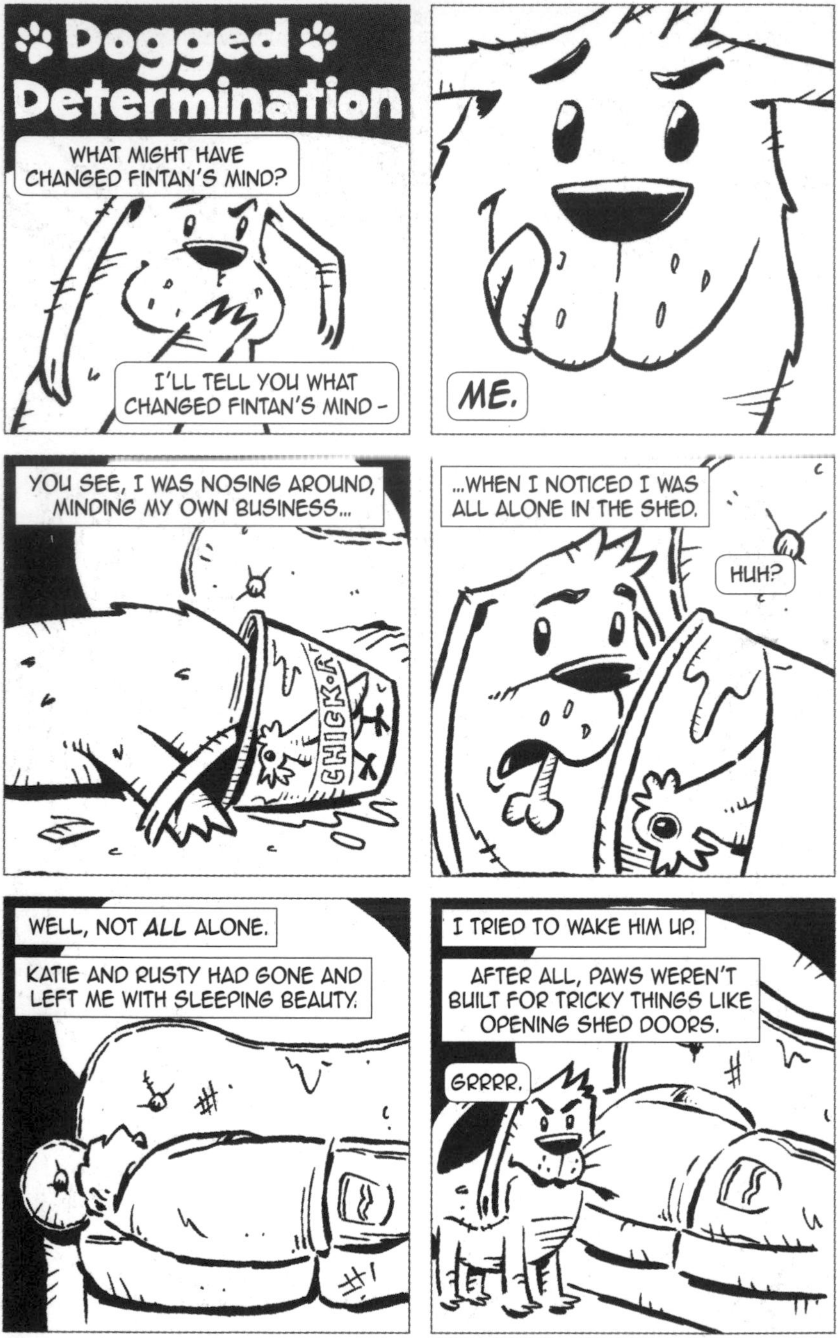
Dogged Determination
WHAT MIGHT HAVE CHANGED FINTAN'S MIND?
I'LL TELL YOU WHAT CHANGED FINTAN'S MIND -
ME.
YOU SEE, I WAS NOSING AROUND, MINDING MY OWN BUSINESS...
CHICK-A
...WHEN I NOTICED I WAS ALL ALONE IN THE SHED.
HUH?
WELL, NOT ALL ALONE.
KATIE AND RUSTY HAD GONE AND LEFT ME WITH SLEEPING BEAUTY.
I TRIED TO WAKE HIM UP.
AFTER ALL, PAWS WEREN'T BUILT FOR TRICKY THINGS LIKE OPENING SHED DOORS.
GRRRR.

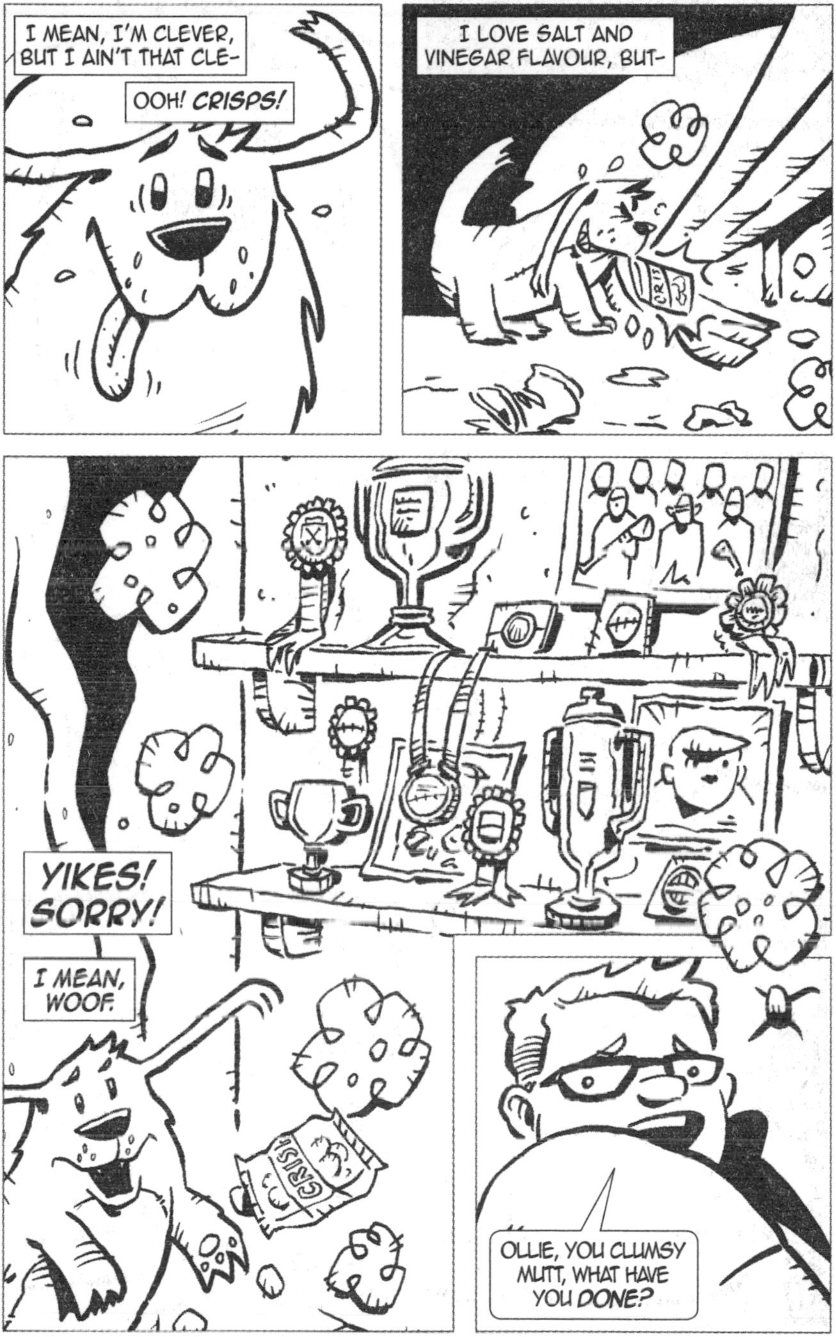
I MEAN, I'M CLEVER, BUT I AIN'T THAT CLE-
OOH! CRISPS!
I LOVE SALT AND VINEGAR FLAVOUR, BUT-
YIKES! SORRY!
I MEAN, WOOF.
OLLIE, YOU CLUMSY MUTT, WHAT HAVE YOU DONE?

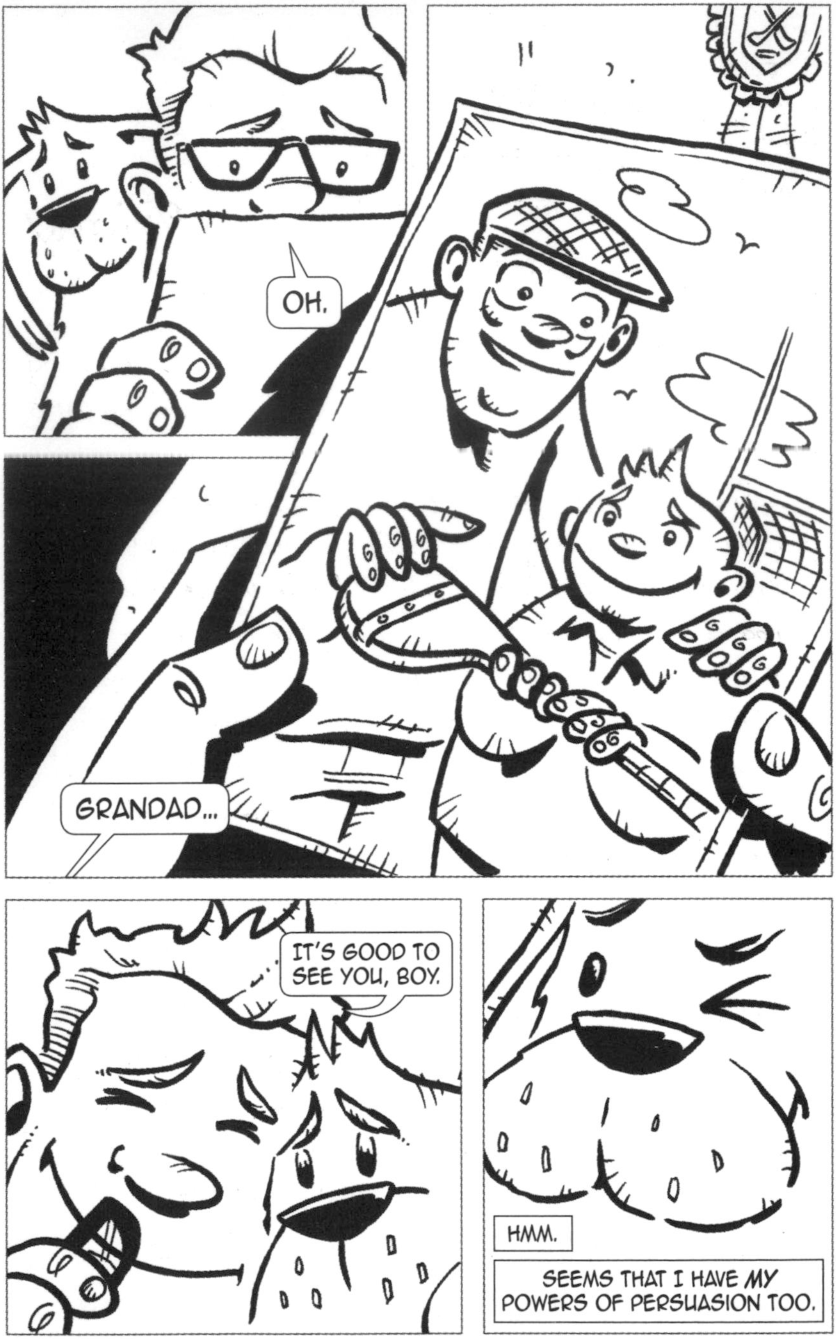
OH.
GRANDAD...
IT'S GOOD TO SEE YOU, BOY.
HMM.
SEEMS THAT I HAVE *MY* POWERS OF PERSUASION TOO.

From the diary of
Seáneen Brannigan,
painter/decorator and
bainisteoir of the
Kilmore Killers U12s
hurling team.

Friday

6pm U12s training
Kilmore Killers

Great training session tonight, Dennis is getting fierce handy with the camán, whacking the legs out from under the man he's marking. Looked like it hurt, but sure it was only Kyle Rogers. He'll be grand tomorrow, and sure he wouldn't be getting a game anyway. Den's got a grand eye for the opportunity, I have to say. He's only eleven now, what kind of savage is he going to be like when he's eighteen?

Funny thing: I was sitting downstairs inside in the lounge earlier on, after the training, reading an article in the paper about the Killers' chances in the league, and there was a big picture of the Lonergan Cup. That battered old piece of scrap metal I wouldn't even use to fix me guttering.

Doreen was watching some rubbish on the TV, something about jewellery - Gemstones In The Attic, I think it was called - aul' ones bring in to the studio their dingy old bits of jewellery that they had stashed down the back of their sofa, and they get them valued by some so-called expert in a flashy suit and a bow tie.

Anyway, this eejit is looking at a necklace that some old lady had brought in and he was getting very excited looking through a magnifying glass at its green-coloured gemstone. 'Ooh, the hairs are standing up on the back of my neck,' he was saying, 'That's one of the lost Evergreen Emeralds, and it once belonged to her Excellency, the Countess of Westmoreland.'

And then there was a bit about the Countess and her emeralds and how she lost them 225 years ago on a trip to Ireland and how there were three of them, two small and one big. All the time I'm watching this on the telly, I'm looking at the paper in front of me and thinking to myself, begob, but that emerald there looks quare like the one stuck slap bang in the middle of the Lonergan Cup. Only much smaller!

Do you know what? I'm sure that big old emerald that belonged to the Countess of Westmoreland has wound up being glued by some dimwit years ago onto the most battered, pitiful old hunk of scrap metal ever to disgrace a winners podium in the history of hurling – the Lonergan Cup!!

Note to self:

check out the Cup next time I'm in Carey Park. And bring a magnifying glass.

Kilmore Killers on Way to U12s Victory

By staff writer Micheál Ferriter

The Lonergan Cup got off to a blistering start this weekend with the Lismore Hackers being decisively beaten 3-2 to 1-5 at home by the mighty Kilmore Killers.

'Daring' Dennis Brannigan lived up to his name, scoring two of the three goals and both of the points in a fantastic display of hurling prowess – he will be one to watch for the future. Kilmore bainisteoir and, coincidentally, Dennis's father Seáneen Brannigan reckons that hurling talent runs in the blood. 'Ah sure, why wouldn't he be a great little player?' he told this reporter, 'wasn't I a great player in my day too? And my father before me?' And who am I to say otherwise? Even at this early stage the Kilmore Killers look to be in pole position to take the Lonergan Cup!

Languishing at the far end of the table are the perennially unfortunate Ballybreen Terriers, beaten with ease by the Castlewilde Wolfhounds and dogged by rumours that all is not too tickety-boo behind the scenes either. And speaking of tickety-boo, was that a ticket to Australia I saw in the back pocket of Ballybreen's bainisteoir Frank Furlong? It seems to me that someone has 'fidgety' feet and may soon be trading in his hurley stick for a didgeridoo…

THE MEN OF IRELAND WERE HURLING WHEN THE GODS OF GREECE WERE YOUNG.

PJ DEVLIN

That Saturday was the Kilmore *Poc Fada* – that's a kind of competition where different players hit a sliotar across country from one place to a finishing point, the winner is the one who gets to the finish line in the fewest 'pocs'. The Kilmore *Poc Fada* starts at the huge, megalithic 'meeting' stone in Kilmore town square, goes up Market Street (be careful of the shop windows and parked cars!), goes out of town, across the fields and up into the hills. The competitor who reaches the dolmen at the top of Barry Hill with the fewest pocs is the winner. I tried it out last year and didn't even come in the top five. It was exhausting – my arms were aching for days after!

The Terriers had booked a minibus to bring us, and we had forgotten to cancel it, so when it arrived only myself, iPaddy, Halfpint, Katie and Ollie the dog were there to 'pile' on.

It felt weird to be on such a big bus, just the five of us, but at least there was plenty of legroom! 'Next time we'll just go in a smart car,' said Katie as she tried to keep Ollie's snout out of the picnic basket.

The *Poc Fada* is usually a great day out, despite being in Kilmore, the home town of U12 hurling's roughest, most accurately named team, the Kilmore Killers. It attracts a huge crowd every year and loads of cash is raised for charity. The Killers' bainisteoir always has his players collecting for their team on the day as well. Fond of a few bob is that man!

Halfpint and iPaddy sat at the back of the bus. iPaddy was listening to his music as usual and Halfpint was doing his best to look out of the window. Not an easy trick when you are less than five feet high. Eventually he had the idea of sitting up on the picnic basket so he could see, which didn't please Ollie in the slightest.

Katie and I sat up front. We hadn't told the lads about our secret, cunning plan for the *Poc Fada* – our secret weapon, you could say. If he turns up!

Soon the bus pulled in to the square in Kilmore. A big crowd was already there – parents and fans, all festooned in their team colours. Katie, eager as ever and excited about our 'secret weapon', was first off the bus. As soon as her feet hit the ground we heard a shout: 'Oi! Dinger!' A tall lad with curly hair and freckles ran up to her and gave her a huge hug. And I mean *huge*. Katie looked shocked. I stepped forward, kind of protectively, but they both started roaring laughing. 'Rusty!' said Katie, 'this is my cousin Rory!'

'Rory Sweeney, at your service!' said the lanky chap in front of me, sticking out his hand to shake. 'But Rory, what are you doing at a *poc fada*?' asked Katie, 'I thought you were into golf?'

'I am,' said Rory, 'I got dragged along by my Uncle Seamus. Mum and Dad are off golfing in Scotland, so I'm staying with Seamus for a few days. He's mad for the hurling, the whole family are. Look, that's my cousin Jimmy there.' He pointed at a short, chubby kid who was wrapping tape around the handle of his hurl, his eyes squinting in concentration. 'He's the craziest about it, he plays for the Castlewilde Foxhounds.'

'The Castlewilde WOLFhounds,' I corrected him. 'They're a good team.'

'I don't see what all the fuss is about, myself,' said Rory. 'You just hit a ball with a stick; it's basically pretty much like golf.'

Sacrilege! My jaw hit the floor! 'There's MUCH more to it than that, Rory, and you know it!' cried Katie. 'He's just messing with you, Rusty. Rory has been playing golf since he was three years old. He's won more trophies than Padraig Harrington and Tiger Woods put together. He's a bit of a golf prodigy!'

A what? I thought to myself. 'Have you ever TRIED hurling?' I asked Rory. 'You should give it a go!' said Katie. 'Yup,' I said. 'If you think all there is to hurling is hitting a ball with a stick, then a *poc fada* would be right up your street!'

'Okay,' said Rory, 'I'll give it a go!' Maybe Rory wasn't so bad after all!

Katie explained the rules to Rory as we walked over to the table to register. The Kilmore Killers' U12 bainisteoir, Seáneen Brannigan was sitting at the table. He sniggered as we approached him. 'Heh, heh. I thought I could get a funny smell, and I just worked out what it is,' he said, looking us up and down, 'the smell of defeat. Tell me now, have you come to disgrace yourselves again, lads, like you did last Saturday? I had my spies at the match, they said yis were all atrocious.'

Halfpint and iPaddy started to growl quietly. 'Say nothing,' whispered Katie. 'He's a big bully – just like his son.'

44

We all knew Dennis Brannigan and what a hard player he was. I still had bruises from our last encounter, and that was the year before! We did as Katie said, and kept our traps shut. The Terriers had our secret weapon, even if most of us didn't know about it.

'And who's this long, lanky stick of licorice with the baseball cap?' asked Seáneen. 'Rory Sweeney, at your–' began Rory. 'I know your uncle,' interrupted the Kilmore bainisteoir. 'He's keen on the hurling alright. But completely rubbish at it. I suppose you'll be the same.' Seáneen sat back.

'Grand stuff. It's a sure thing for my Dennis, so.'

'We'll see about that,' I whispered to Katie.

Rory was fuming. 'Who was that obnoxious man?' he asked. 'The Kilmore Killers' coach,' said Katie. 'Biggest bragger in the competition, with a team full of dirty players.'

Rory, Halfpint and I took our places at the starting line. Katie and iPaddy joined the crowd to cheer us on. Katie was saying something to iPaddy, but of course he couldn't hear her over the din from his headphones.

'Ready for the Terriers to get beaten again, Rust-bucket?' said a voice from beside me. It was Dennis Brannigan. He brushed his blonde fringe out of his eyes and gave me a sneaky dig in the side with his hurl.

'I wouldn't be so sure of that,' I said, looking down the row of contestants to where a large boy was joining late. He wore a baseball cap low over his eyes and a tight-fitting Ballybreen Terriers jersey. 'Who's that now,' said Dennis. 'Nobody you know,' I replied. From the sidelines, I caught Katie's eye and she grinned and winked at me. Our secret weapon had arrived! I looked at Rory, 'Let's go.'

Dennis was first up. He threw his ball in the air and gave it a mighty whack. From the crowd I could hear Katie and iPaddy groaning. The poc was good, the sliotar ending up halfway up Market Street. Seáneen shouted, 'Good man, Dennis! Give it socks!'

Then the lad on the end with the Terriers jersey hit his first sliotar. The ball flew nearly all the way up Market Street, straight and true. A cry went up from the crowd and they started applauding. The lad just pulled the brim of his baseball cap down further over his eyes. Beside me, Dennis's head whipped around. 'Wow,' he said, 'who's that in the Terriers jersey?' 'Haven't a clue, must be a new guy,' I replied and gave my own sliotar a whack. My ball only went half the distance of Dennis's poc, but I didn't care.

Our 'secret weapon' looked out from under his brim and gave me a half smile and a nod. I smiled back at him, gave him a quick thumbs-up and mouthed silently, 'Nice one… Fintan!' He winked and pulled his collar up to hide his face better.

Katie and iPaddy cheered my effort, but shut up in pure shock when Rory Sweeney, despite never even holding a hurl before, hit his ball almost as far as Fintan had. 'Huh. It must be all the golfing practice,' he said to me over Katie and iPaddy's surprised cheers. I shook my head in disbelief. We already had Fintan back leading the Terriers, we had to get this guy Rory on board as well!

We all hit our sliotars again – this time our secret weapon, Fintan, and Rory went way ahead of me, Halfpint and the other contestants. Only Dennis was coming close to the two of them, and he didn't look happy about it at all, probably wondering where these two clowns had come from, one in a Terriers jersey and one some golfing cousin of Dinger Bell! By the next poc Dennis was as far behind the two as the rest of us. They were really flying. I could hear the crowd asking themselves who the big guy in the Terriers shirt was and laughed to myself. Even iPaddy beside me had no idea it was Fintan, and I wasn't going to ruin the surprise.

Up the hills we went, following after Rory and Fintan. Then Rory hit his sliotar an almighty smack and it landed right at the base of the dolmen. The crowd cheered, not believing that a novice could win the Kilmore *poc fada* in twelve pocs! The guy in the Terriers jersey looked at the sliotar in his hand, turning it over, then he threw it high in the air and whacked it with his hurl. The sliotar flew up and came down, hitting the top stone of the dolmen and bouncing into the grass. It landed right beside Rory's ball. He had taken just twelve pocs to do it as well – it was a draw! The crowd went crazy, running up to the two of them and shaking their hands.

Rory looked surprised to be one of the winners, but it was nothing compared to the surprise the crowd got when the big lad in the tight-fitting Terriers shirt took off his baseball cap and revealed himself to be Fintan Lonergan. A shocked silence descended for a moment, and then the crowd went really wild! They shook Fintan's hand and clapped him on the back so much I thought his hand might fall off and that he might need surgery on his spine!

Halfpint and iPaddy were in shock. But a happy shock.

'Fintan's back,' I told them. 'And I've asked him to manage us.'

I thought Halfpint was going to faint. 'That's … that's brilliant!' he said. 'Sorry, what was that?' asked iPaddy, taking his earphones out.

'I'm going to be your new bainisteoir,' said Fintan as Ollie jumped up on him, licking his face. 'And the first thing I want to do as manager is … to get this guy on the team.'

'Me?' said Rory, 'but I've never played before.'

'Anyone who can hit a ball like that, whether it's a golfball or a sliotar, has the makings of a great hurler,' said Fintan. 'Are you game?' Rory looked at Katie and the rest of us. 'How could I let my favourite cousin down?' he said, 'I'm in!'

We all cheered and the Ballybreen Terriers, all seven of us (including Katie and Ollie the dog) made our way back to the minibus.

Seáneen and his son Dennis walked behind us, and I could feel Dennis's eyes burning into our backs as Seáneen gave out to him in angry whispers. They didn't look at all happy that Fintan Lonergan had returned to the Ballybreen Terriers. *Good*, I thought.

SHEEP IN A HEAP.

BABS KEATING

We met up again on the Monday evening after homework for our first training session under Fintan. Despite the good feeling of the Terriers' success at the *Poc Fada*, the session did NOT go well. It was lashing rain and, I have to admit, the four of us on the pitch were clumsy and out of shape, missing passes and shooting wide of the goal as we slipped and slid on the wet grass. Only Rory could hit the ball in anything resembling a straight line, even though he turned up for training wearing spiked golf shoes and a pastel coloured, diamond-patterned sleeveless jumper.

Fintan watched from the sidelines with Katie beside him. Katie was shivering under an umbrella and Ollie was sheltering at her feet.

'Okay, okay, lads,' shouted Fintan, coming on to the pitch with rain pouring down his face, 'Let's leave it there and talk tactics in the clubhouse.' We trooped after him into the leaking metal container. 'Holy moley,' said Fintan as he looked around. 'I was going to give you a talk about your strengths and weaknesses and all that kind of stuff, but I think the first thing we need to do as a team is to do something about this clubhouse. I don't think this place has had a lick of paint or even a sweep of the floor since I was playing.' The others nodded in agreement. The place was a horrible mess.

I put up my hand. It felt silly, Fintan was less than a year older than me, but he felt to me to be much older, like a teacher … or a bainisteoir. 'Fintan,' I said, 'my dad is a carpenter, I could ask him to maybe put in some proper benches, some hooks and stuff like that?'

'Brilliant idea!' shouted Fintan.

'I could get my uncle Seamus to paint the walls,' said Rory.

'Fantastic!' cried Fintan.

Halfpint piped up, 'My brother's an electrician, I could ask him to look at the wiring.' 'That's exactly what we need!' said Fintan. 'We can't be training out of a disgusting kip like this, no wonder the team is depressed!'

'Well, let's get started on it now,' said Katie. 'No time like the present. And it's too wet to train anyway.' She was right, it was bucketing down. We got busy cleaning instead.

As we tidied up, throwing rubbish into black plastic sacks we found in a cupboard and sweeping up with a brush that had less bristles than Seáneen Brannigan's bald head, Fintan appraised our performance on the training pitch. He had a way of giving us bad news in a nice way. 'Look, lads,' he said, 'on the training pitch there, I see great potential. Your last bainisteoir mustn't have been training you hard enough, or maybe just not training you in the right ways, that's all. Your playing is, well, kind of soft and flabby.'

'You can talk!' said Halfpint. 'Halfpint! That's not nice!' cried Katie, but Fintan held up his hand. 'He's right, Katie.'

Fintan went quiet then for a while, and sat down on the arm of the battered sofa. The sofa lifted up slightly at the other end. 'You know,' he said, 'that's the reason I gave up hurling two years ago – my weight. Mam said it was just puppy fat, but I couldn't shift it. It wasn't slowing me down, it made no difference to my game, but … I dunno, I just didn't look like myself. I'd look in the mirror and … and it was like I didn't know the boy who was looking back at me. Then, in the final. You remember, Katie? The final two years ago against the Kilmore Killers, we were going great in the first half, 2 points ahead at the break. Even that old bainisteoir we had back then, Sulky Sullivan, was happy. But when we came back out on the field it started. You fellas couldn't hear them. They were careful not to let you. The Killers started coming up to me on the field and whispering to me.'

'Whispering what, Fintan?' asked Katie.

'Fat,' said Fintan, whispering himself now. He closed his eyes and looked down. '"Fat boy. Fat eejit. Fat Fintan".' He sighed. 'I was only ten. I was only small. Well, I was big, but you know what I mean.' We smiled despite ourselves. '"Fat Fintan". It broke my concentration. I couldn't hit the sliotar straight. The hurley felt like it was made out of lead. I started sweating. I ... I just couldn't play anymore.'

Katie slapped the back of the sofa hard. 'Those thugs.'

'So,' said Fintan, 'I quit. Right after the match I told Sulky I wasn't coming back. He tried to talk me around, but I was sick. Sick to my stomach.'

'But, Fintan, WE never–' said Halfpint quickly.

'I know you didn't, lads, I know you didn't. And I'm sorry I let you down. That won't happen again. You know, it took me a long while, but I realised that, well, everyone is different. Some people are tall, some people are short.' Halfpint giggled a bit and Ollie licked him. 'Some wear glasses – I need them myself for reading and playing video games – some aren't great at school, some have big ears, big noses, big feet … and some are fat. And you know what? They're all GRAND. I'm happy to be the way I am. We weren't all meant to be the same, it'd be a boring 'oul world if we were.' Fintan stood up and cleared his throat. 'So, with that in mind, I think it's time to cast our net wider if we want to find some players for the team. They don't have to be great hurlers, not at first anyway. They just have to be team players. And most of all, they have to be happy to hurl!'

The Old Dog for the Hard Road

OH, YEAH, *I* REMEMBER THAT MATCH AGAINST THE KILMORE KILLERS LIKE IT WAS YESTERDAY.

IT WAS HALF TIME AND I REPAIRED TO THE KILMORE CLUBHOUSE IN SEARCH OF SOME SUSTENANCE.

...WHEN I HEARD OL' SEÁNEEN BRANNIGAN IN FULL FLOW, GIVING HIS TEAM A GOOD TALKING TO.

IT SEEMS HE WASN'T TOO HAPPY THAT THE BALLYBREEN TERRIERS HAD THE ADVANTAGE.

YIS PACK OF DESPERATE GOOD-FOR-NOTHINGS! THE TERRIERS *ARE TWO POINTS AHEAD!*

THAT *LONERGAN* KID IS RUNNING RINGS AROUND YE!

BUT HE'S TOO FAST TO CATCH, MISTER BRANNIGAN!

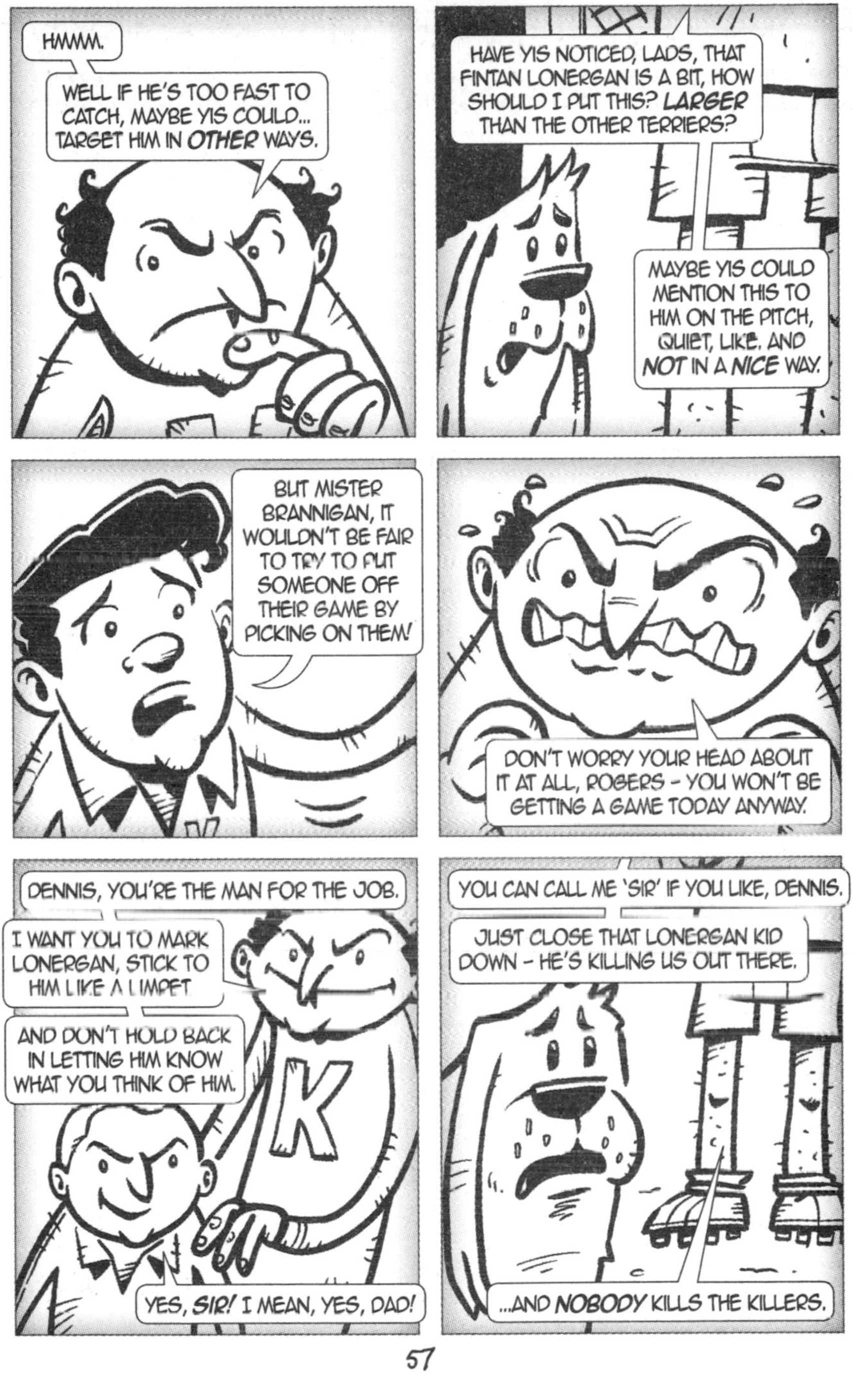
HMMM.
WELL IF HE'S TOO FAST TO CATCH, MAYBE YIS COULD... TARGET HIM IN OTHER WAYS.
HAVE YIS NOTICED, LADS, THAT FINTAN LONERGAN IS A BIT, HOW SHOULD I PUT THIS? LARGER THAN THE OTHER TERRIERS?
MAYBE YIS COULD MENTION THIS TO HIM ON THE PITCH, QUIET, LIKE. AND NOT IN A NICE WAY.
BUT MISTER BRANNIGAN, IT WOULDN'T BE FAIR TO TRY TO PUT SOMEONE OFF THEIR GAME BY PICKING ON THEM!
DON'T WORRY YOUR HEAD ABOUT IT AT ALL, ROGERS - YOU WON'T BE GETTING A GAME TODAY ANYWAY.
DENNIS, YOU'RE THE MAN FOR THE JOB.
I WANT YOU TO MARK LONERGAN, STICK TO HIM LIKE A LIMPET.
AND DON'T HOLD BACK IN LETTING HIM KNOW WHAT YOU THINK OF HIM.
K
YES, SIR! I MEAN, YES, DAD!
YOU CAN CALL ME 'SIR' IF YOU LIKE, DENNIS.
JUST CLOSE THAT LONERGAN KID DOWN - HE'S KILLING US OUT THERE.
...AND NOBODY KILLS THE KILLERS.

I WOULD RATHER HAVE GREYHOUNDS THAN ELEPHANTS.

JIMMY BARRY-MURPHY

The next day after the Monday training was sunny, and Fintan, Katie and I went to Ballybreen public gym. Not to train again, but to watch a wrestling match, of all things! Fintan had heard that there was an eleven-year-old guy who went by the name of Dominic 'Mansize' McLean competing in the match, and that he might be interested in hurling. I could see why he had the nickname 'Mansize' – for an eleven year old, he was HUGE! He was at least five foot ten, and he slammed his much smaller opponent easily onto the mat, time and time again.

After Mansize had won his match and sent the smaller competitor wandering off with his ears ringing and his tail between his legs, Fintan went over to him. 'So, I hear you're thinking of taking up hurling?' he said. 'Aye,' said Mansize in a rich Scottish accent, 'I am that.' We introduced ourselves, and Fintan told him all about the team, about Katie being our number one fan and about me being from Brazil and only taking up hurling in the last year. 'So, you see, it's never too late to take up hurling – I did, and I love it!' I said. 'You're from Brazil, are ye?' said Mansize, 'that's great. I'm an immigrant too – all the way from sunny Inverness.' 'I didn't know Scotland was sunny,' said Katie. 'Ach, I'm only kiddin' ye,' he said with a booming laugh. 'It buckets down all the time in Scotland. That's why I feel so at home here in Ballybreen!'

Mansize told us that back in Scotland he used to compete in the Junior Highland Games. 'Aye, I used to love the hammer throw and tossing the caber – you know, hefting up a big log and seeing how far you could throw it. Like this.' He took a heavy punch bag off its holder, hoisted it up in his arms and tossed it halfway across the gym floor. It must have weighed six stone, but he made it look as easy as throwing a tissue. This guy was STRONG! 'But you see,' said Mansize, 'they're all solo sports. Just like wrestling. I'd like to try out a team game.'

'Well,' said Fintan, 'we may be able to help you out.' Mansize agreed to come along to our next training session on the Thursday night

Fintan had another trip for us on the Wednesday evening, this time to the far side of Ballybreen. Katie and I cycled over to the Primrose Meadows estate at the edge of town and met Fintan at the gates as he was being dropped off by his mum. 'I've a mate who lives in number seventeen,' he said. 'I met him through online gaming – you know the game "Chicken Detective"? It's about these chickens in San Francisco and–'

'And they're detectives?' smiled Katie.

'You DO know it!' said Fintan. 'Well, anyway, I met Liam through that game. We were partners in the Chicken Detective Unit and we solved–' Katie and I were looking at each other with our eyebrows raised. Fintan looked embarrassed. 'Well, it doesn't matter. Anyway, Liam is a grand chap. I met up with him last year. He's very sporty and I'm sure he'd be into a bit of hurling. And he has certain … skills …'

Fintan pushed the doorbell of number seventeen and the door opened, seemingly all by itself. Fintan stuck his head in. 'Hello? Liam?' Suddenly there was a whoop from the top of the stairs and a small figure slid at lightning-quick speed down the banisters, launched himself off the bottom of the stairs and performed a perfect double somersault in mid-air before landing on his feet like a particularly nimble cat. 'Ta dah!' he said.

'Fellas,' said Fintan, 'this is Liam Chang.' I looked at the small lad in front of us. He was only slightly taller than Halfpint, skinny, with a mop of jet black hair and as fidgety as Fidgety Furlong – this guy was a bundle of energy!

'I know you,' I said. 'You work on Saturdays in the Euro Store in Shop Street.'

'My family OWN the Euro Store,' said Liam. 'And I know you. You are the year ahead of me in school.'

'Liam's family moved to Ballybreen last year,' said Fintan. 'They used to travel around the country with Denny's International Circus.'

'We are acrobats! The Flying Changs!'said Liam proudly, scratching his head with his toes. 'Well, we used to be. Before Dad got injured and we settled down and opened up the shop. Mum says I have to take up a sport. She says I've too much, you know, energy, since we gave up acrobatics.'

'I told him he has to stop swinging out of the light fittings and get out from under my feet,' said Mrs Chang, coming out of the living room and grabbing a wriggling Liam by the shoulders to keep him still. 'Hurling would be good for him, Fintan. Thanks for asking him along!'

'No problem at all, Mrs Chang! We'll see you tomorrow night so, Liam?' 'Cool beans,' said Liam.

We all laughed. Two new players in two days! Cool beans, indeed!

Terriers in Tatters

By staff writer Micheál Ferriter

Well, well, well. The U12 Ballybreen Terriers are starting to look like the dogs who have had their day. Rumours of bainisteoir Frank Furlong's departure for 'down under' seem to have been true – a little kookaburra bird has told me that he went walkabout after their disastrous defeat to the Kilmore Killers on that stormy Sunday a couple of weeks ago, prompting most of the team to follow suit. 'Fidgety' Furlong is now whacking his sliotar up and down Bondi Beach, with the Terriers just a distant, bad memory. And the Terriers themselves? What's left of them look to be in tatters. They can't come back from a calamity like this, can they? You heard it here first: the Terriers are finished.

The Kilmore Killers, on the other hand, are going from strength to strength. Following their win over the Ballybreen Terriers (Knock Knock. *Who's there?* The Ballybreen Terriers. *The Ballybreen Terriers who?* That's hurling!), the Killers decisively beat another pack of dumb dogs, the Castlewilde Wolfhounds, last Sunday 4-12 to 0-14. If the Killers can keep up this winning streak, no team (dogs, cats, humans or otherwise) can stop them taking the Lonergan Cup!

MAY THE BEST HORSE JUMP THE DITCH AND WE WILL SEE WHAT HAPPENS.

DAVY FITZGERALD

Our first match with Liam Chang, Mansize McClean and Rory came around quickly. So quickly that we weren't ready for it in the slightest – we weren't even on time for the throw-in! The Dunbrogan Badgers were on the pitch and the referee was looking at his watch and just about to declare a no-show when the three people-carriers carrying the Terriers arrived. We fell out of the cars and ran towards the pitch. We could hear the Badgers' fans laughing as the plastic bag holding the water, juices, after-match treats and packets of crisps split wide open while Katie was running, spilling its contents onto the grass, but the crowds' laughter was silenced when they saw the last person to appear!

Fintan Lonergan hopped down out of the people carrier and calmly strode towards the pitch as a hush descended on the crowd. The Badgers' bainisteoir shushed his team. 'C'mon now, lads. Fair play. Let's give the Terriers a few minutes to get themselves together.' 'A few minutes? They look like they need a few weeks!' said one of the Badgers, but their bainisteoir held up his hand. 'Put a sock in it now, Tom.'

Fintan spoke briefly to the referee who started laughing, and then shook hands with the Badgers' bainisteoir. 'It's good to have you back, Fintan,' said the Badgers' manager, clapping him on the back. 'It's good to BE back. I think,' said Fintan. 'Are you good to go?' asked the referee. 'Well, I'd say we're as good to go as we're going to get,' replied Fintan. 'Rusty, you're captain.' I gulped.

The ref blew his whistle and play started. Embarrassment has wiped my memories of that first match with the new Terriers team, but it's enough to say that we did NOT play well. All I can remember is that Rory hit the sliotar the length of the pitch (and further, out of play) on several occasions, Liam was very fast and lively, but couldn't hold the ball on the bas of his hurl to save his life, Mansize was like a walking brick wall, knocking over Badgers and giving away free pucks left, right and centre. At half time we were two goals and seven points down. It was not looking good.

We came off the pitch dejectedly. Fintan was sitting on the grass with his head in his hands, but suddenly he sprang to his feet. For a big guy, he was surprisingly fast-moving. He looked at us and smiled. 'Okay, lads. We're not going to win this one – we've only been training since Wednesday and Liam only joined up two days ago. But I'll be happy if we can walk off the pitch with a point. It'd be a great start to the new Terriers. We could walk off the field with our heads held high. I'd be delighted, I'd be ecstatic. And if one of you scores a goal, I'll … I'll …'

'What will you do, Fintan?' Halfpint asked excitedly.

'Alright. If one of you lads scores a point, I'll take off my jersey and do a lap of the pitch.' 'In your vest?' said one of the younger lads. 'I'm not wearing a vest,' said Fintan. 'No vest, no jersey, one

lap of the pitch for one point. Have we a deal?'

'Deal!' we shouted and all cracked up. The three new boys smiled and looked at each other. I laughed and jumped up, ready for action. 'You're on, Fintan. C'mon lads, let's give it a lash.'

The second half went a bit better. We were still very sloppy –
Liam Chang crashed into the immovable slab of muscle that was
Mansize McLean and had to sit down for a few minutes until his
head cleared, and iPaddy kept tripping over his own feet while
marking his more nimble opponent, landing awkwardly on his
backside more than a couple of times. But we were all smiling and
had actually forgotten we were losing the game! All we could think
of was getting the point that would make Fintan have to live up to
his promise. I tried to marshal the troops as best I could, but the
three new guys were inexperienced (although enthusiastic!) and
the younger guys were all about six inches shorter than even the
smallest Dunbrogan Badger.

I looked over at Fintan at the sideline. He had Katie and Ollie
on either side of him, but he looked worried, biting his nails. I
wondered if he was regretting his rash decision to do a jersey-less
lap if we scored a point, especially as the last game he had played
in, the last game he had actually been to, he was bullied about
his weight. Mind you, it didn't look as if we were going to score
anything, so it looked like he was safe enough.

But when I watched the Terriers on the pitch I realised that for
the first time in a long time they were actually starting to have fun!

They knew we hadn't a hope of winning, but they were all having a great time chasing that point. The game had turned into exactly that – a game, not a battle. When we stopped worrying about how we were playing, our passing started to improve, we were defending better, stopping the Badgers from getting anymore points or goals of their own. Mansize was magnificent, so big that no-one was getting past him, a natural defender.

We were seconds away from the final whistle when iPaddy passed the sliotar to me, I caught it neatly and whacked it up and ahead blindly as hard as I could. It fell by pure chance directly into the path of one of our younger players, a squirt called Phil Tutty (he was almost as small as Halfpint) and Phil swung his hurl, made contact and sent the sliotar spiralling high, up and over the Badgers crossbar! We had scored a point! Phil Tutty was more surprised than anyone – he hadn't got a touch of the ball until that moment! The official's arms went up, signalling it was a clean point and the final whistle blew.

The Terriers fans erupted in cheers. Well, I say erupted, there was only Katie, Ollie and a couple of the mums and dads that drove us. The team ran up to me and we hugged, laughing with exhaustion and relief. It was like we had won the match – in fact, that one point felt better than a win! This was the first time we had enjoyed a match for as long as any of us could remember.

Fintan joined us on the pitch and wordlessly removed his jersey. To astonished looks from the crowd and to the thunderous cheers of the Terriers, he ran a slow lap of the entire pitch, his arms upraised. He was out of shape, but he never slowed down to catch his breath, and when he got back to us he wasn't even wheezing slightly. He put his jersey back on and we clapped him on the back.

'Well done, lads,' he said. 'That point was as good as a goal any day.'

The Terriers were back!

From the diary of
Seáneen Brannigan,
painter/decorator and
bainisteoir of the
Kilmore Killers U12s
hurling team.

Sunday

one o'clock match -
Dunbrogan Badgers V
Ballybreen Terriers

Well, if I hadn't seen it, I wouldn't have
believed it. I thought we got rid of that
Lonergan kid years ago, but there he was
today at the match. Of course, the Terriers lost, they're hopeless - I just went to
check out the Badgers.

The Terriers seem to be giving a few new
fellas a run out. Some of them actually
didn't look too bad, but they were still being beaten like the losers they are. Then the
weirdest thing happened. Just at the end of
the match they scored a point - a lucky ball
came down in front of the goal and they just
fumbled it over the bar. But that wasn't the
weird thing.

At the end, that Fintan fella threw off his
jersey and ran bare-chested around the pitch!

And that big belly of his flappin' around —
the half-baked eejit.

All of the team were smiling though, looking
like they were having a great time. I'll have
to keep an eye on that.

Update on the emerald situation

I went to Carey Park to have a look at the
Lonergan Cup. It was behind glass in the
trophy cabinet so I couldn't get too close,
but, begob, that green stone looks like the
yoke off the telly — the lost Evergreen Emerald. I had a photo of the one that turned
up that I found on the internet and this one
looks like an exact match. I'm going to have
to come up with some sort of a plan to get
my hands on it...

HURLING IS THE RIVERDANCE OF SPORT.
LIAM GRIFFIN

At the next training session after the Dunbrogan match the mood was good. We were still laughing to ourselves about Fintan's lap of honour, and Phil Tutty was the man of the hour, being the point-scorer. Fintan gathered us together on the pitch and said he had an announcement to make. *Holy moley*, I thought, *He's giving up on us already*. But Fintan smiled broadly and said, 'Okay guys, I've decided to ask Katie to help out coaching the Terriers.' Katie took her place beside Fintan, she looked delighted and proud. 'Don't worry, we'll be doing all the usual stuff,' continued Fintan. 'The warm-up, the passing practice, the running and the like. But Katie will be bringing in a few training exercises taken from her own interests and her own sports that will be a bit different and you might enjoy.'

'Okay, boys,' said Katie, 'my sports are hockey and tennis, and you know I'm a majorette as well.' 'Go, the Ballybreen Spinners!' shouted Rory. Ollie barked excitedly. 'And the most important thing in all those sports is balance. Without a good sense of balance we wouldn't be able to keep the sliotar on our hurls or keep our feet when we're marking our man. iPaddy. iPaddy!'

iPaddy took one of his earphones out. 'Huh?' 'iPaddy,' Katie continued, 'you have to take off your headphones when you're playing; they're affecting your balance.' iPaddy looked dismayed, 'But I can't live without my music, man.'

'The noise is affecting your inner ear and that's what controls your balance,' Fintan explained. 'No wonder you spent more time sitting on the grass than hurling in the last match. You'll just have to sing to yourself in your head from now on.'

'So,' said Katie, 'today we're going to do some balance exercises.' Fintan brought over a sports bag that clanked as he walked. Katie unzipped the bag and we found out what the clanking noise was as Fintan handed around big tablespoons. Katie followed behind him, handing us each an egg from a family-size box.

'Right, lads,' she said, 'for the first balance exercise we're going to do an–' 'An egg and spoon race?' interrupted Halfpint. 'Oh, it's much harder than just an egg and spoon race!' she said as Mansize appeared behind her, hefting a huge sack. 'An egg and spoon race … on skateboards!'

Five minutes later we were over at the roadway beside the pitch, each of us holding an egg on a spoon and wearing a safety helmet as we balanced precariously on skateboards. 'Be careful of the boards and the helmets,' said Katie, 'they have to be back in Rory's Uncle Seamus's shop first thing tomorrow morning.'

'And be careful of the road,' said Fintan. 'It's full of potholes!' Katie put a whistle to her lips. 'Okay, ready, set, GO!' She blew the whistle and we kicked off on the skateboards with the eggs on the spoons, flying down the potholed road.

Pretty soon the yolk was on US!

A Couple of Bow-Wow-Wowsies!

THE SKATEBOARD EGG AND SPOON RACE WASN'T THE ONLY WEIRD EXERCISE THE TERRIERS DID THAT DAY...

...ALTHOUGH IT WAS THE MESSIEST.

KATIE TAUGHT THEM *MAJORETTE* TRICKS...

WAY-HEY!!

...AND SHE ROPED IN RORY TO GIVE THEM A FEW GOLF TIPS.

THIS'LL BE GREAT FOR WHACKING THE –

WHAT'S IT CALLED AGAIN?

THE SLIOTAR.

– FOR WHACKING THE SLIOTAR A LONG DISTANCE.

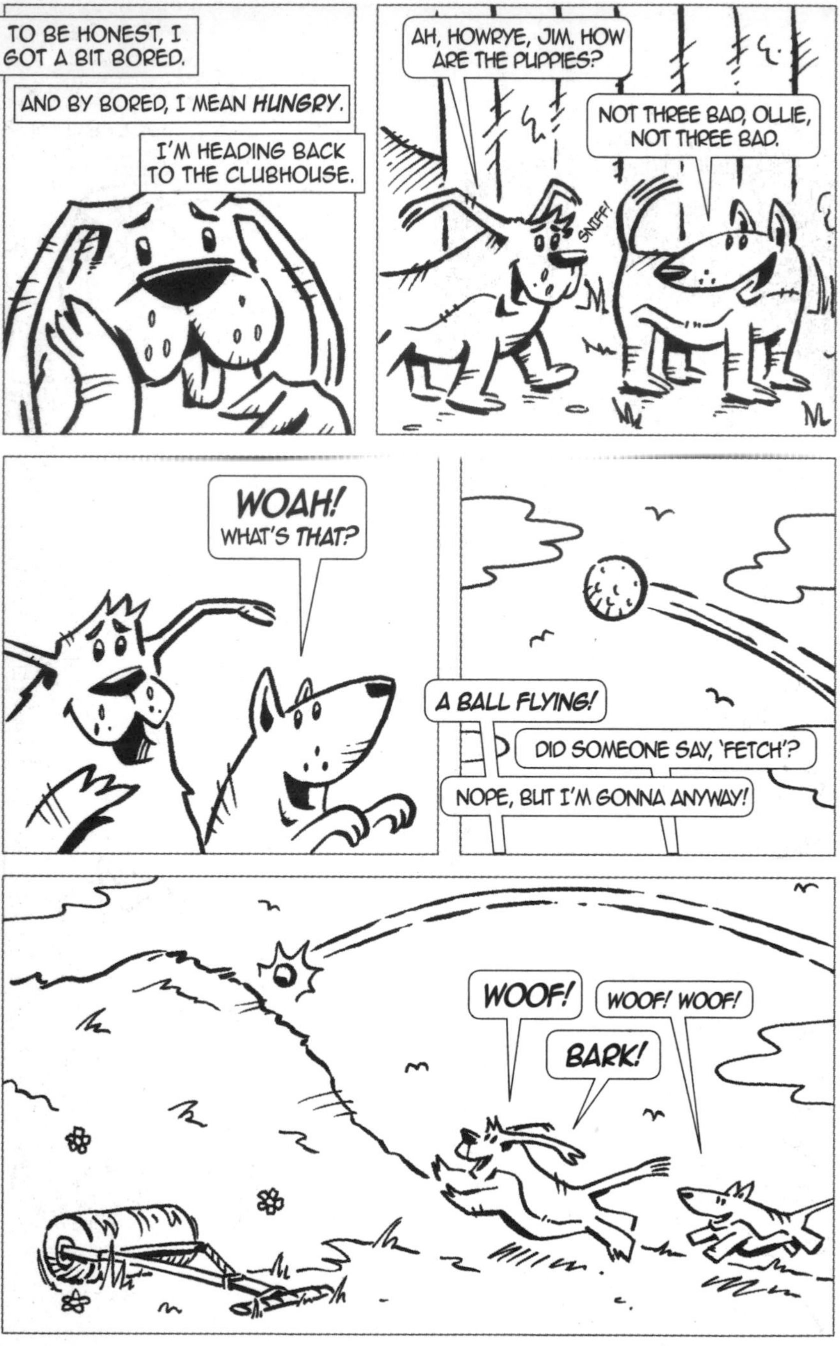
TO BE HONEST, I GOT A BIT BORED.
AND BY BORED, I MEAN HUNGRY.
I'M HEADING BACK TO THE CLUBHOUSE.
AH, HOWRYE, JIM. HOW ARE THE PUPPIES?
SNIFF!
NOT THREE BAD, OLLIE, NOT THREE BAD.
WOAH! WHAT'S THAT?
A BALL FLYING!
DID SOMEONE SAY, 'FETCH'?
NOPE, BUT I'M GONNA ANYWAY!
WOOF!
WOOF! WOOF!
BARK!

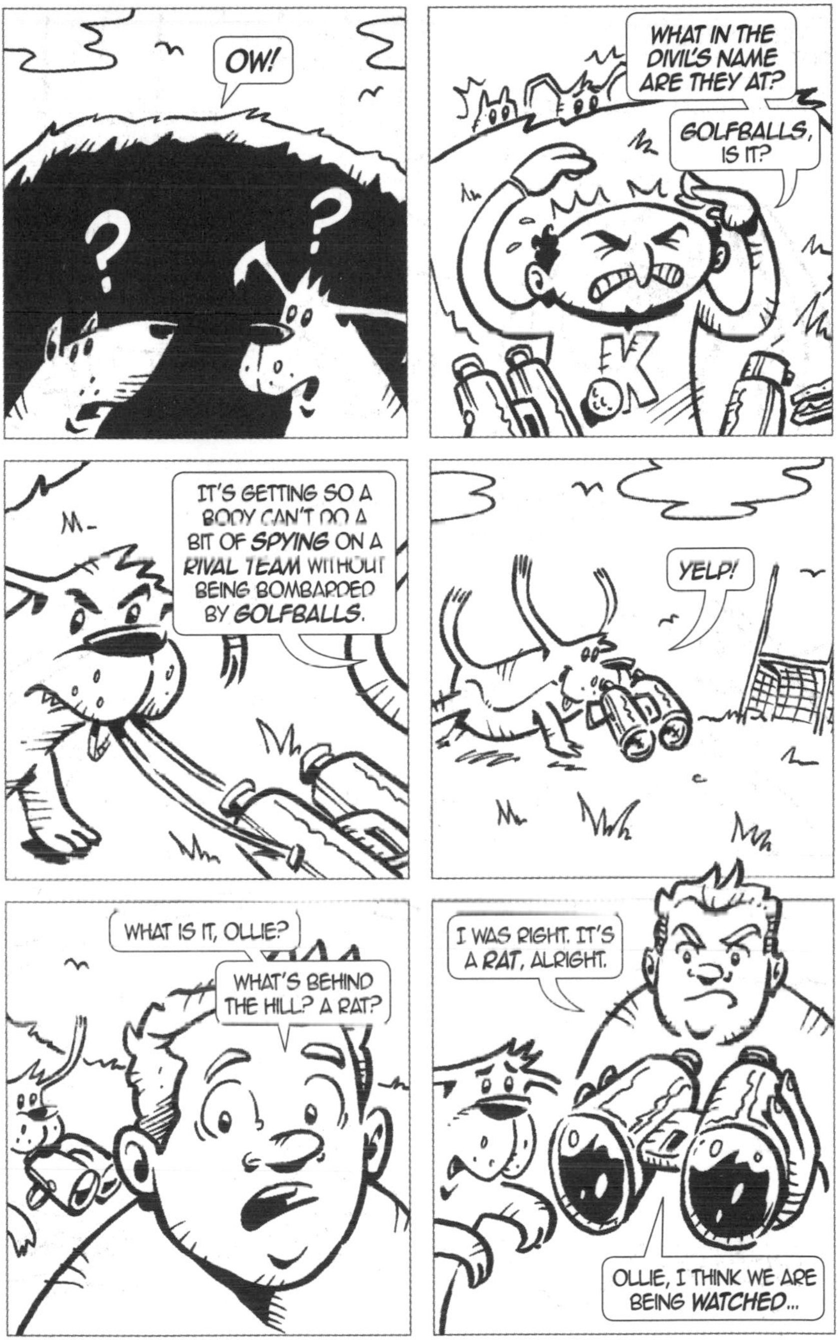
OW!
WHAT IN THE DIVIL'S NAME ARE THEY AT?
GOLFBALLS, IS IT?
IT'S GETTING SO A BODY CAN'T DO A BIT OF SPYING ON A RIVAL TEAM WITHOUT BEING BOMBARDED BY GOLFBALLS.
YELP!
WHAT IS IT, OLLIE?
WHAT'S BEHIND THE HILL? A RAT?
I WAS RIGHT. IT'S A RAT, ALRIGHT.
OLLIE, I THINK WE ARE BEING WATCHED...

I ALWAYS LIKED TO DO THE IMPOSSIBLE.

CHRISTY RING

A Dublin lad, Henry Gupta, came to Terriers training a couple of days before our next match, against the Lismartin Hackers. Henry used to be goalkeeper for a soccer team when they lived in Dublin, but had given up playing when his family moved to Ballybreen. His parents were accountants and were not fans of soccer, hurling, or any sport. They'd prefer Henry to be working in the family accountancy firm in the evenings after he'd finished his homework, but Henry had seen that the Terriers were recruiting from posters that Fintan and Katie had put up in Dempsey's supermarket in Shop Street and he was dying to have a go. The only problem was that he was a very shy type of lad, and I heard later on that it took him four training sessions before he got up the courage to actually come into the field and knock on the clubhouse door.

He needn't have worried; Fintan gave him a great welcome. 'Listen,' he told Henry, 'it doesn't matter if you've never played before. Every new player brings something new to the training pitch. Give it a go – you'll never regret picking up a hurley!'

The match against the Hackers was at home, and we were very glad that we had cleaned up the clubhouse! We had scrubbed off all the rust and painted it a lovely, bright, fire-engine red – the Terriers' colours! Inside was all dickied up as well, with new benches and fittings, all thanks to various mums, dads, uncles, aunts and siblings. We were very proud of our new, improved clubhouse, and also very proud of the pitch, which was in good order for the first time in months with good, green grass and hardly any muddy puddles.

The Hackers let us know they meant business just seconds after the throw-in, scoring a point almost from their first touch of the sliotar.

But we meant business too! Our new training regime, along with Fintan's tactics sessions (all chalked out on a blackboard we found in a skip behind Ballybreen National School) were beginning to pay off. Katie and Fintan's enthusiasm, as well as the arrival of the new players, had had a huge effect on our performance as a team. We were enjoying the game for the first time in years! Hurling made us feel good, and feeling good about ourselves made us play better and made us want to get stuck in!

I opened up the scoring for the Terriers with a lucky ball over the bar, set up by Halfpint. Then, the improbable happened – Rory Sweeney scored a goal! Right from the Terriers' own goal mouth, right the way up the pitch and through the legs of their goalkeeper, who was fast asleep and thought all the action was down the other end.

It was! The Terriers went crazy, slapping Rory on the back as he stood goggle-eyed, gaping in disbelief at what he had done. Fintan, Katie and Ollie were dancing, shouting and howling from the sideline with Henry Gupta. I could see that Katie had her eyes shut tight and her fingers crossed.

'Right, lads,' shouted Fintan. 'Capitalise on this! Get up the pitch and get us another!'

If we were surprised by Rory's goal, the Lismartin Hackers were utterly bewildered! This wasn't supposed to happen – nobody concedes a goal to a luckless bunch of washouts like the Ballybreen Terriers! We ran up the pitch to the halfway line and I swear they took a couple of steps back from us. They were completely rattled! Play resumed again, and although we played with confidence and huge smiles on our faces, the Hackers got a couple of points back before half time.

'We've got to hold what we have,' said Fintan as we drank water from little plastic bottles at the side of the pitch. 'We defend from here on, keep the Hackers to their own half as much as possible, and keep possession of the ball.'

He turned to Liam and Halfpint. 'But that doesn't mean we're not going for a win today! Liam and Halfpint, you're the smallest and fastest. I want the other guys to give you cover. If there's points to be had, or even,' he crossed his fingers like Katie, '… or even another goal, Liam and Halfpint will be the ones to get them. But if any of you other lads see an opening, go for it! You are all brilliant, lads! Now, get out there and get the win!'

We started the second half defending, with nearly all of us in our half. The Hackers tried coming at us mob-handed, but a few of us twirled our hurleys around, as if they were batons, spinning them until they became blurs in our hands and slowing the Hackers down. Katie gave us the thumbs-up sign from the sideline, delighted that we were putting her majorette moves to good use. The Hackers scored another point, but you could tell they were shaken by the Terriers' unexpected confidence and new-found skills. They barely cheered.

Then the impossible happened twice! Rory hit the sliotar from far back in our own half again – a good, straight shot, all he was short of was shouting 'Fore!' Liam had sprinted unnoticed up the pitch to a sweet spot in front of the Hackers' goal. Rory's shot dropped perfectly into Liam's path and, with only the keeper to beat, Liam swatted the ball over the unfortunate keeper's left shoulder and into the goal. While we were going crazy for the second time, the whistle blew and we realised that we had WON THE MATCH!!

Fintan and Katie flew onto the pitch and flung themselves on us. Ollie jumped around, barking excitedly, and was hugged by Henry. Mansize started to cry and had to be comforted by Katie. Fintan and the rest of the team hoisted Liam and Rory onto our shoulders. We couldn't believe it. We had actually won a match!

Terriers Turnaround?

By staff writer Micheál Ferriter

Well, here's a turnip for the books! Last weekend this reporter found himself present at an historic and very rare occasion in local U12s hurling history – the Ballybreen Terriers won a match! Despite the fact that the win was against the not-very-highly-fancied Lismartin Hackers, it was undoubtedly a major achievement for the up until recently beleaguered Terriers, and for their new bainisteoir, the very young Fintan Lonergan, who obviously has been working wonders for the team on the training pitch. And if you think that name sounds familiar, it's because Fintan has played previously for the Terriers and his family name graces the Lonergan Cup.

New boys Liam Chang and Rory Sweeney distinguished themselves, scoring a goal apiece, leaving the final score an incredible 2-1 to 0-3. The Terriers played with enthusiasm and passion, and were obviously enjoying themselves, but the big question on everybody's lips is – can the Terriers repeat this kind of high-energy performance in their next match against the Kilpedder Crusaders, or was this scoreline a complete fluke?

Meanwhile, the Kilmore Killers haven't lost a match yet, confidently beating the Rathfinn Dolfins 3-1 to 0-2 at home. I bet Seáneen Brannigan has dusted off a place on the Kilmore mantelpiece specially for the Lonergan Cup already.

From the diary of
Seáneen Brannigan,
painter/decorator and
bainisteoir of the
Kilmore Killers U12s
hurling team.

Thursday

Training 6pm

What are those Ballybreen Terriers at?

The original plan was to win the division and win the cup. And then I'd get my hands on the Evergreen Emerald! But these eejits are throwing a Spaniard in the works. The way it was looking, it was shaping up like the Kilmore Killers would be up against the Athleague Athletes in the final. The Athleague ATHLETES!

I've never heard of a club so badly named – half of them are over 13 stone and the rest of them huff and puff if they have to get up out of a chair in the morning, they couldn't be less athletic if they tried. We could have beaten them with our eyes shut and our camáns made out of cardboard. Not that we wouldn't have beaten the Terriers as well. At least, we would have until recently.

I've seen their training techniques and they're nothing less than farcical.

But they seem to be doing the trick. We can't bet on winning against that chubby lad and his mismatched pack of gobdaws by using just brute force. No. If I want to get to that cup, it'll have to be before it's handed out. But it's safely stowed away in the trophy cabinet in Carey Park, how would I ever get in there? Hmmmm...

Note to self:

Call Jimmy Breslin, the Carey Park manager tomorrow morning and offer him a good deal on painting his office and maybe the trophy room? Make him an offer he can't afford to refuse.

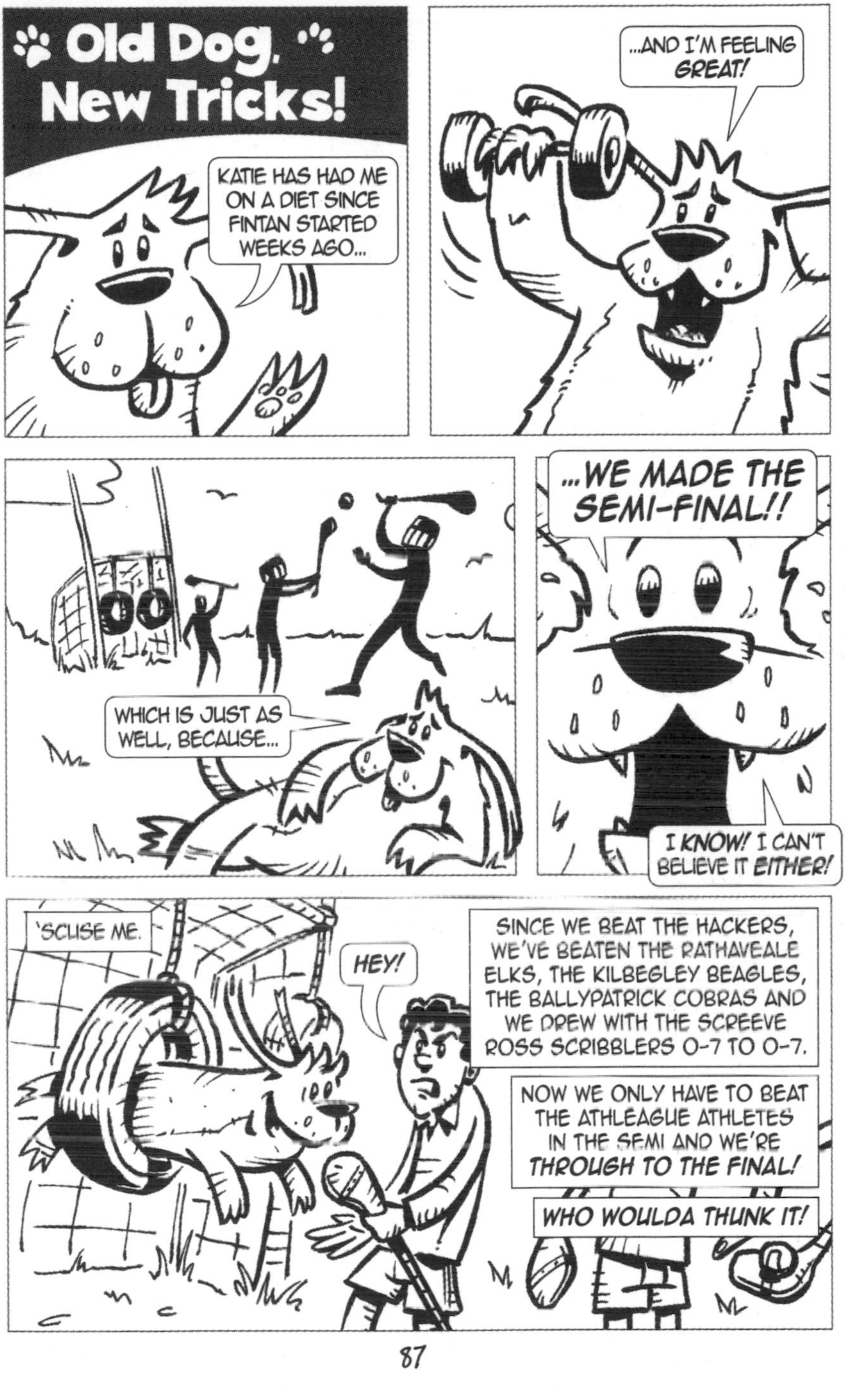
Old Dog, New Tricks!
KATIE HAS HAD ME ON A DIET SINCE FINTAN STARTED WEEKS AGO...
...AND I'M FEELING GREAT!
WHICH IS JUST AS WELL, BECAUSE...
...WE MADE THE SEMI-FINAL!!
I KNOW! I CAN'T BELIEVE IT EITHER!
'SCUSE ME.
HEY!
SINCE WE BEAT THE HACKERS, WE'VE BEATEN THE RATHAVEALE ELKS, THE KILBEGLEY BEAGLES, THE BALLYPATRICK COBRAS AND WE DREW WITH THE SCREEVE ROSS SCRIBBLERS 0-7 TO 0-7.
NOW WE ONLY HAVE TO BEAT THE ATHLEAGUE ATHLETES IN THE SEMI AND WE'RE THROUGH TO THE FINAL!
WHO WOULDA THUNK IT!

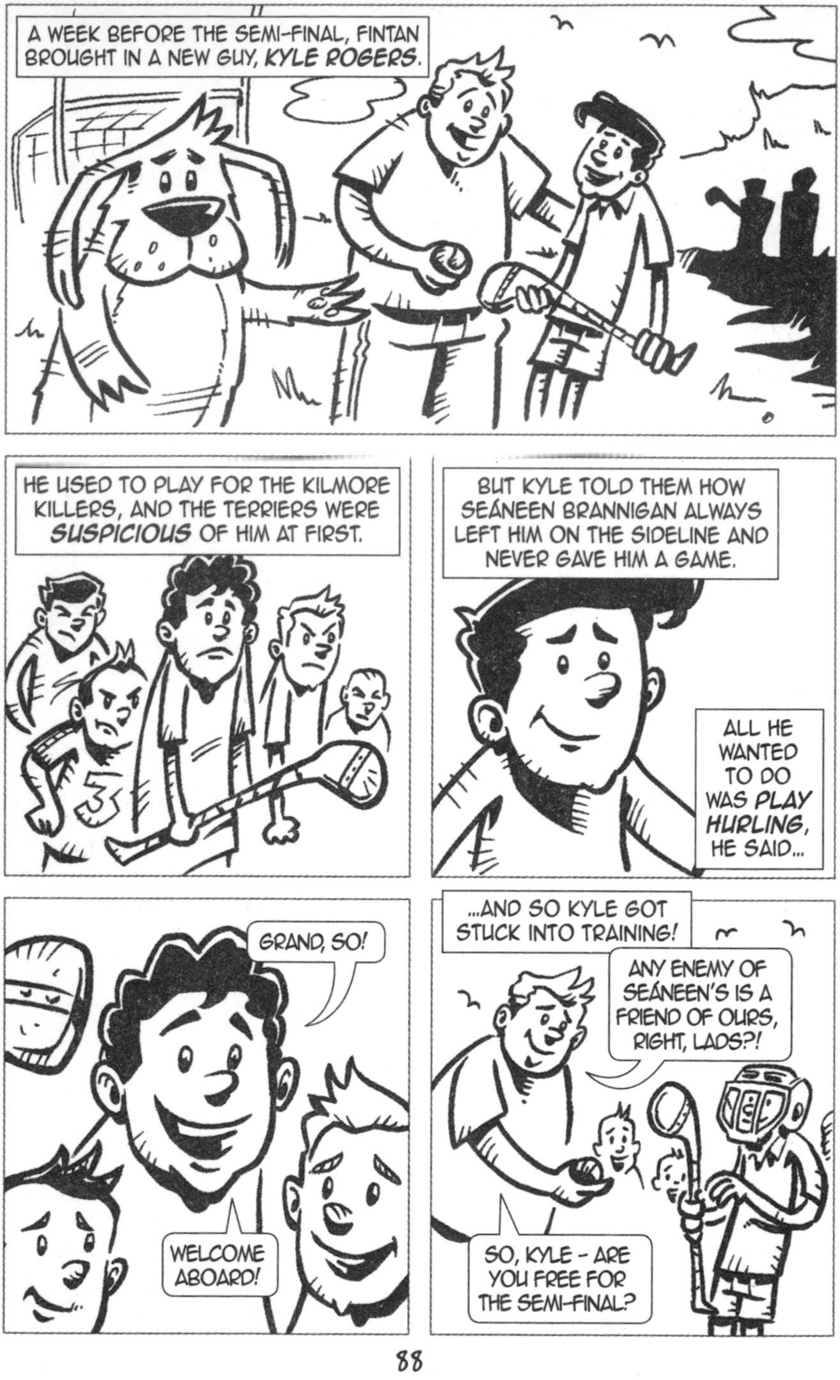
A WEEK BEFORE THE SEMI-FINAL, FINTAN BROUGHT IN A NEW GUY, *KYLE ROGERS*.
HE USED TO PLAY FOR THE KILMORE KILLERS, AND THE TERRIERS WERE *SUSPICIOUS* OF HIM AT FIRST.
BUT KYLE TOLD THEM HOW SEÁNEEN BRANNIGAN ALWAYS LEFT HIM ON THE SIDELINE AND NEVER GAVE HIM A GAME.
ALL HE WANTED TO DO WAS *PLAY HURLING*, HE SAID...
GRAND, SO!
WELCOME ABOARD!
...AND SO KYLE GOT STUCK INTO TRAINING!
ANY ENEMY OF SEÁNEEN'S IS A FRIEND OF OURS, RIGHT, LADS?!
SO, KYLE - ARE YOU FREE FOR THE SEMI-FINAL?

HE GRABS THE SLIOTAR, HE'S ON THE FIFTY... HE'S ON THE FORTY... HE'S ON THE THIRTY... HE'S ON THE GROUND.

MÍCHEÁL Ó MUIRCHEARTAIGH

I knew Kyle to see, but had never seen him play because Seáneen Brannigan always seemed to leave him on the bench. It turned out that he was a nice lad and a very good hurler, with a nice touch and a keen eye for a high ball. But as nice as he was and as good at hurling as he was, the other lads in the team seemed wary of him. 'Once a Kilmore Killer, always a Kilmore Killer,' I heard one of them say. Kyle didn't mind them, he just wanted to play.

Fintan asked him to look after our goalkeeper Henry Gupta, the newest member of the squad, and to help him with extra training and give him a few tips. Kyle was delighted, and him and Henry had a great laugh at that training session, with Henry becoming less shy and more chatty as the hours went by.

Finally, Fintan blew his whistle. 'Well, lads,' he said, 'the next match is the semi-final. If we go out on that one, there will be no shame. You have done brilliantly to get this far.' We smiled and nodded to each other, we still couldn't believe how far we'd gotten. 'But I believe you can go a bit further. The Athleague Athletes are a great team, but they're a bit slow because they're all bigger lads. Like me. It must be all the butter they make in Athleague.'

I looked at Fintan. He was wrong to say that he was as big as the Athleague boys. Fintan had been training as hard as we had for the last couple of months. He had lost a lot of weight and looked a different person to the lad who had become our young bainisteoir when the team were at our lowest ebb. He stood tall now, not quite as tall as Mansize McLean, but as well-built as Mansize was and just as full of energy. He was fit as well, as fit as any player on the Terrier team, and his former self, the lad with the greasy jumper and the half-eaten bucket of fried chicken, was just a distant memory.

'Do you know what I think,' he said, 'I think we can beat Athleague, I really do. And I think that we better get onto our mams and dads and uncles and aunts and get them to buy their tickets for the final!'

We cheered loudly and Ollie howled.

We were still cheering as our minibus arrived at the Athleague pitch for the semi-final. We had been singing on the bus all the way from Ballybreen. Only Fintan had been quiet, lost in his own thoughts at the front of the bus.

The match started well, and we were up five points in the first twenty minutes, mainly thanks to Rory (who had become a great player, once he learnt a couple more skills as well as his 'golf swing' move) and to Mansize, who was the most 'solid' defender any team could ask for.

But, just when you are at your most confident, disaster has a habit of striking. We conceded six points to the Athletes quickly in the second half and the boys looked anxious, beginning to look like they were losing their nerve a little. It's funny how quickly a team can become used to winning, and falling behind one point had shaken us up. We really didn't want to lose this one, we had come so far.

Towards the end of the second half, Liam Chang found himself hovering around the Athleague goal completely unmarked. He moved so fast it was hard for the opposing defenders to keep track of him. Close to our goal, a high sliotar fell onto iPaddy's hurl and he legged it up the pitch towards Liam. Because iPaddy had left his headphones in his kit bag he had nothing to distract him and easily outpaced the heavier, slower Athleague players. But as he reached the halfway line he picked up a tail – one of the smaller Athletes was hot on his heels. I shouted to him to watch his back, but the player behind him stuck out his hurl, bringing off a nasty tackle and sending iPaddy crashing to the ground. Despite his helmet, iPaddy got a pretty hard knock on his head. If he was a cartoon he would have had stars and little tweety birds flying around him! Fintan and Katie rushed onto the field and carried him off to the sidelines where he sat, moaning.

Kyle Rogers came on then, running enthusiastically onto the pitch. He was running around the Athletes' goal mouth with plenty of energy in his fresh set of legs. Kyle kept calling for one of his new teammates to pass him the ball, but the Terriers seemed reluctant – they didn't trust him – after all, he was a Kilmore Killer. The sliotar came to me and I sent it in Kyle's direction. Kyle bounced it once on the bas of his hurl and whacked it effortlessly past the Athleague keeper and straight through the posts for a goal. Looking relieved, he quietly clenched his fist in a little expression of victory. The Terriers went wild, cheering and clapping Kyle on the back. Whatever he was before, Kyle was a Ballybreen Terrier now!

And if the Terriers went wild at Kyle's goal, they went completely bonkers four minutes later when the full time whistle sounded. We had made the final! Kyle was the hero of the match, and Katie hugged him hard. As the Terriers celebrated, I noticed Fintan sitting down heavily on the grass a lttle bit away from us, with Ollie beside him. 'We did it,' he said quietly to himself. 'We did it.'

The bus back to Ballybreen was held up while Fintan was being interviewed by Micheál Ferriter for the local rag, but when he eventually boarded, a huge cheer went up. We had all worked hard over the last few months, but we all knew that it was Fintan who had gotten us here, it was Fintan who was the inspiration behind all our wins, it was Fintan who brought the fun back into our game. Katie sat down beside me and, to my surprise, kissed me on the cheek.

'That was a great idea of yours to get Fintan back,' I said, blushing a bit. 'Yup,' she said, 'but he wouldn't have stayed if it wasn't for you.'

Fintan stood at the top of the bus. He looked at us all for a long moment as we sat in silence.

'Next week,' he said, 'THE FINAL!!'

From the diary of
Seáneen Brannigan,
painter/decorator and
bainisteoir of the
Kilmore Killers U12s
hurling team.

Thursday

Training 6pm, last one
before final!!

Well, we beat those Lismartin whelps in the
semi and we're through! I KNOW we're going
to beat the Ballyhreen crowd on Sunday, I've
no doubts there. But JUST IN CASE we
don't, I have put my plan into action to get
my hands on that cup by hook or by crook.

You see, I went to see Jimmy Breslin, the
Carey Park manager and gave him some guff
about being the Kilmore bainisteoir, as well
as being a respected painter and decorator,
I'd like to give something back to the com-
munity that had given ME so much, and yadda
yadda yadda. I offered to paint his office -
AND the trophy room - free of charge. And
guess whut? He fell for it. I said I'd do it
over the weekend, Saturday and Sunday. 'Saturday and Sunday?' says he, 'Won't your
team be playing in the final?'

'They will,' says I, 'But sure, don't they know what they're doin' at this stage? I'll be lookin' out the window of the trophy room to keep an eye on them.'

And here's the genius part, when I came in to size up the room for the painting last week I took a few pictures of it. AND I took a few pictures of the cup while he wasn't looking... all the better to HAVE A COPY MADE! That's right, I went to that dodgy jeweller fella over in Derrybeg and got him to make me up a copy from the photographs. He's not doin' too bad a job either.

It's not an exact replica, but it'll pass muster - in the excitement of the win, nobody will notice that I will have been in the trophy room and will have swapped the priceless cup for the one that cost me 40 quid, and that the cup that went back into the trophy cabinet is the Euro shop version! I'll have that Evergreen Emerald prised out of the Lonergan Cup, tell everyone I found it in the attic like yer man on the telly, and I'll be stinking, disgustingly RICH!!

And the best thing of all? Win or lose, that tubby thickhead Fintan Lonergan, his family of has-beens, and his team of half-baked freaks WON'T KNOW A THING!

Terriers Triumphant?

By staff writer Micheál Ferriter

Over the last few short months the Ballybreen Terriers have, incredibly, gone from strength to strength under the stewardship of the league's youngest manager, Fintan Lonergan. I caught up with Fintan after his team's recent win over the Athleague Athletes and asked him about his surprise return to hurling, the Terriers' shock semi-final placing, getting through (against all odds) to the final itself, and how it feels to be 'top dog' with the Ballybreen Terriers.

Micheál Ferriter: Fintan, the change in the Terriers' fortunes since you came on board has been amazing. How did that come about?

Fintan Lonergan: Well, Micheál, I had been out of hurling for a couple of years, as you know, when one day, out of the blue, Katie Bell arrived at my house with Rusty Arantes and they asked me to come back. I was unsure at first, but seeing Katie, and Ollie, our mascot, made me realise how much I missed the game, how much I missed being part of the team, and how much I owed hurling.

MF: Your family have a great tradition of hurling, haven't they? The Lonergan Cup itself is named after your grandfather.

*FL: Yes, it is. My granddad was a great man and a great hurler –
he played for his county. He was the driving force behind hurling
in the area and donated the Cup. It was just a family heirloom we
had in the attic, but it looked nice polished up. Katie and Rusty
reminded me why I never should have given it up.*

MF: There are many rumours as to why you quit the game two
years ago.

FL: I quit for personal reasons, but I'm back now.

MF: You're back and looking fit!

*FL: I've been training with the team. Katie has come up with
some great training games and we've all enjoyed ourselves.*

MF: You certainly looked like you were enjoying yourself today,
that was a great win over the Athletes. I've never seen the Terriers
play so well, what do you put that down to?

*FL: When I started with the Terriers as manager, I saw the
biggest problem they had was lack of self confidence and
enthusiasm. They were beaten down by being beaten so often,
and we'd lost half the team. I decided to bring in players from
different sports but who fancied hurling. 'Pick up a hurley, it'll
never let you down,' I used to say. The arrival of new players
with all their new skills kind of energised the team and got them
thinking. And Katie was a huge help there, with recruiting
and training. I think the Terriers were always winners, even
when all the other teams had written us off. We just got out of the
habit of enjoying the game.*

MF: And what about the final? Can the Terriers go all the way?

*FL: The Kilmore Killers and the Lismartin Hackers are both
very strong teams, we'll just do our best and enjoy it. Win, lose
or draw, the most important thing in hurling is to have fun and
enjoy the game!*

Spoken like a real champion.

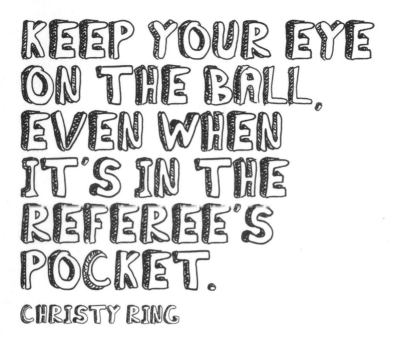

KEEP YOUR EYE ON THE BALL, EVEN WHEN IT'S IN THE REFEREE'S POCKET.

CHRISTY RING

The day of the final at last! We met up in the Terriers' clubhouse an hour before the match at Carey Park. Since we had done it up, the clubhouse looked fantastic – it was hard to remember how rotten it had looked only a few months earlier as it sat there now with its new Terrier-red paintjob gleaming in the sun. Some of the mums had hung red and yellow bunting from its flat roof, and even Ollie's kennel was decorated in the Terrier colours. Katie's mum had made a little red coat for Ollie and he paraded around proudly, looking every inch the Ballybreen Terrier mascot!

Before we left for Carey Park (in a coach this time, not in a half-empty minibus), Fintan stood before the assembled players, mums and dads, brothers and sisters, uncles and aunts and beaming friends. He held his hurley stick in his hand and the thought struck me that I couldn't remember the last time I saw him without it.

He cleared his throat and a hush came over the assembled crowd. Lined up in a row at the front, the players all looked at him expectantly. He opened his mouth and paused for a long moment. Then he smiled the biggest, widest, most delighted smile I have ever seen.

'Terriers,' he said quietly, 'let's go.'

We sang in the coach all the way to Carey Park!

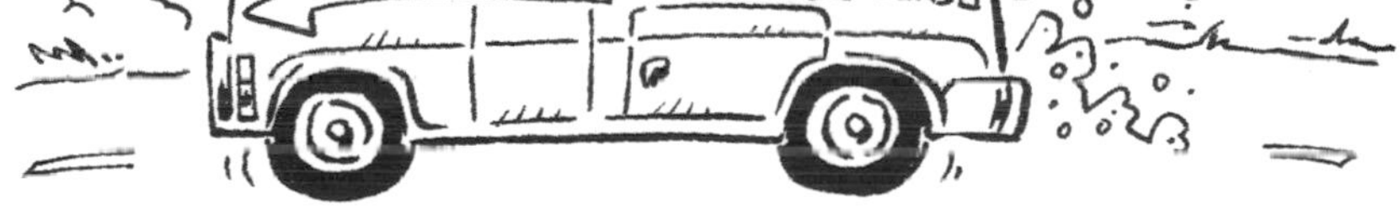
O'BRIEN TOURS

On the coach, though, Fintan sat alone, and he was the last one to get off. The team had run on ahead in their excitement, but Katie and I walked with Fintan to the dressing rooms.

'Last minute nerves,' he said. 'Don't tell the others.'

'Don't worry, Fintan,' I said, 'didn't you read your own interview in the paper? This is meant to be fun!' 'Yeah,' he replied. 'You're right.' He smiled and Katie laughed as Ollie strained on his lead, barking happily. Fintan slapped me on the back and strode towards the dressing rooms. 'C'mon guys,' he said, 'let's have some fun!'

Katie joined the Ballybreen Spinners majorettes who were marching with the Kilmore National School Band for the National Anthem before the match and they both put on a great show, the Spinners throwing their batons high in the air and the band only playing the odd bum note.

After the anthem the Kilmore Killers came over to us. 'Holy moley,' said Dennis Brannigan to Fintan, a sneer on his sneaky-looking face. 'Where did you get this bunch of goons from? I've never seen a crew of misfits like this in my whole life!' 'Yeah,' piped up the tall goalkeeper, Michael Winkles, 'Chang isn't the only one of you who'd look at home in the circus!'

'Ignore them, lads,' said Fintan, never taking his eyes from Dennis. 'We may be a mixed bunch, but we're all the better for it. You'll find that out on the pitch, Dennis. And as for you, Winkles, if you keep hearing whooshing sounds, they'll be the noise our sliotars make as they fly past your ears!'

'Heh,' said Dennis, 'we'll see, chubby boy.' Mansize McLean growled, drew himself up to his full height and stepped up beside Fintan. Seáneen Brannigan appeared out of nowhere quickly. 'Ah,' he said, 'what Dennis means is, best of luck, may the best team win.' He sneered a very similar sneer to his son. 'And WE will.' He looked at Fintan, his eyes flashing. 'The Terriers winning the Lonergan Cup? FAT CHANCE!' Then Seáneen laughed and turned his back to us. He and his team walked off up to their own end, the Killers throwing us filthy looks all the way. 'Right, then,' said Fintan after a few moments. He clapped his hands. 'Let's win this game and bring that Lonergan Cup home!'

The most important sixty minutes of our lives started at a very gentle pace. After the throw-in the Kilmore Killers kept the ball for a long while, handpassing it between their half-backs and midfielders. We were chasing the sliotar around from Kilmore player to Kilmore player, getting frustrated as we tried to find a way in, when suddenly one of their midfielders whacked the ball up the pitch to Dennis Brannigan who struck it towards our goal. The break came so quickly and the ball was so fast that Henry Gupta, fine goalie that he was, hadn't a chance of stopping it. It flew past his ear into the net and the green flag went up.

Seáneen Brannigan did a little dance on the sidelines, thrusting his fist into the air. 'Great going, lads!' he was shouting. 'And remember, when ye get the sliotar, hit it like ye hate it! Do ye hear me? Hit it like ye hate it!'

We inwardly groaned at the goal but outwardly cheered only two minutes later when iPaddy, earphone-less yet again for the big occasion, slammed the ball over the bar at the other end! That shut Seáneen up!

The Killers then started to play dirty. After the puckout, Dennis held onto the sliotar, keeping both the ball, and the referee's attention, down near the Terriers' goal. Up at the other end of the pitch, four of the Killers decided to knobble Liam Chang, barrelling into him at the same time. Poor Liam hit the ground to shouts of 'Foul!' from the crowd, but as the referee turned to see what the commotion was, Dennis slapped the ball past Henry a second time. I picked up Liam from the grass. His helmet was a bit askew, but he was fine.

In fact, Liam had seen the four Killers bearing down on him

and ducked quickly just as they reached him, causing two of the Killers to clash helmets – one of them looked a bit dazed. 'Serves them right,' said Liam, more determined than ever to score. And he did, just five minutes later – Rory struck the ball with one of his trademark long-range golf-style swings of the hurley right the way up the pitch from the Terriers' goal to the Kilmore goal. The ball bounced once in front of Liam and he whacked it past their keeper!

When the whistle blew for half time the scoreline was Terriers

1-1 Killers 2-O. Katie and Ollie were waiting for us in the dressing room, and Fintan walked in behind us and stayed standing as we sat down on the wooden benches. 'Lads, you're doing brilliantly,' he said. 'I've been trying to think of what to say to you all today. And it's this: Thanks. Thanks for bringing me back to the Terriers. Thanks for reminding me how much I love the game.'

He sat down on the bench, and we leaned in to listen to him in complete silence. 'Before Rusty and Katie came around to my house to persuade me to come back, I was ... well, I was lost. I was sad, and lonely, and unhappy, and I didn't even know it. All I did was play video games, watch movies and stuff my face. But Rusty and Katie came around and put the hurley back in my hand and I remembered what I was born to do. I was born to be a Terrier, just like my father and grandfather before me. Ballybreen is my town and the Terriers are my team. And you guys, you're not just my friends, you're my brothers. Win, lose or draw today, nobody can take that away from any of us. The Terrier blood flows in our veins!'

And with that he jumped to his feet and let out a huge, dog-like howl! Ollie joined in, and then so did the rest of us, all howling our heads off, Katie included!

'Ho-ho-hooooooooooooowwwwwwwwwwlllllllllllll!!!'

Seáneen Brannigan stuck his head in through the door to see what the commotion was, but quickly ducked back out and disappeared up the corridor. Ollie sniffed the air and padded after Seáneen, but the rest of us Terriers stayed in the dressing room, howling and laughing until we had to go back to the pitch for the second half.

In the second half, the Kilmore Killers were up to their tricks again. Seáneen had obviously told them at half time to take out our best players, and they did so with relish, crowding out me, iPaddy, Liam Chang and Halfpint with brute force and dirty play. The Killers were a bigger team than us, full of big, tall lads, and

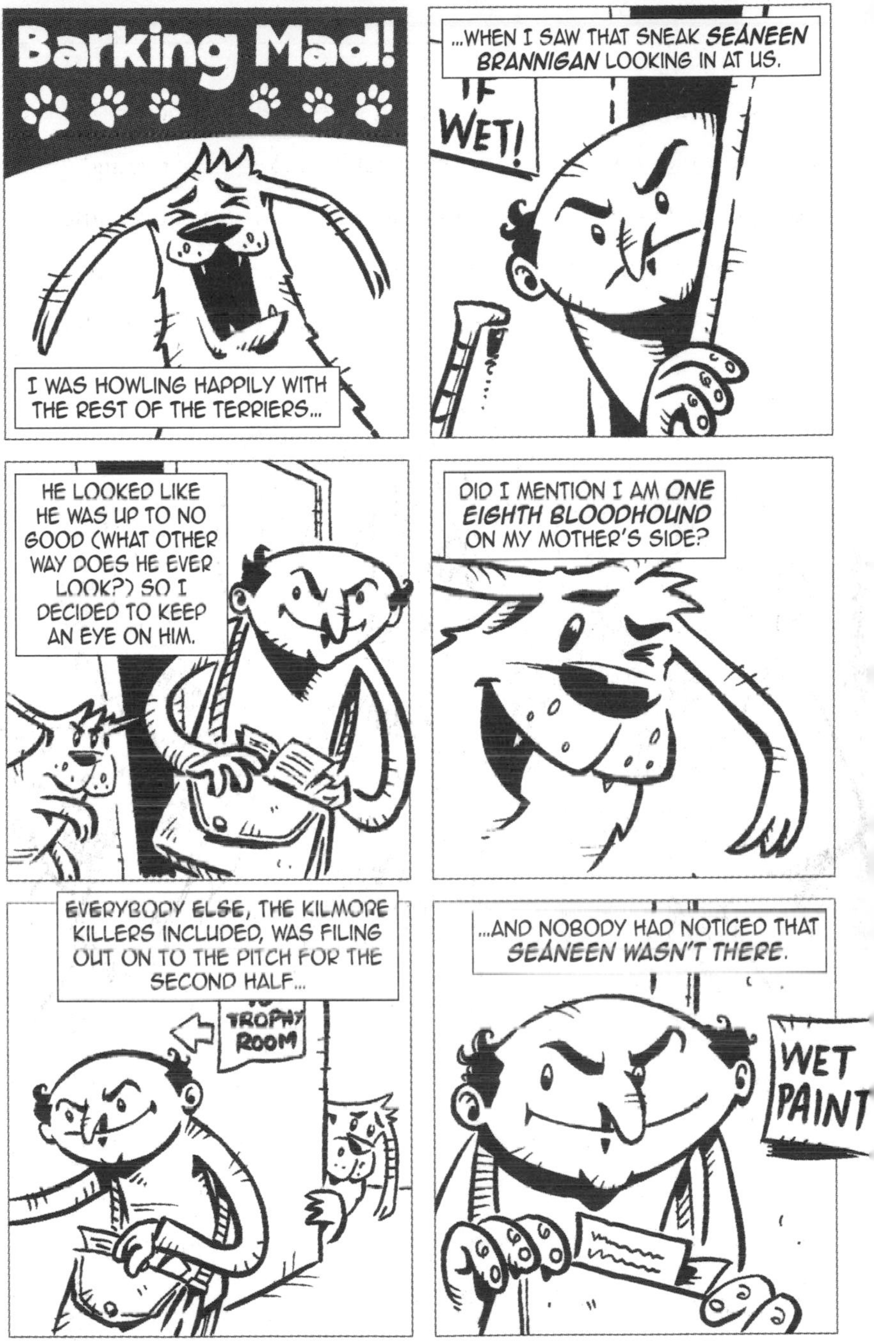
Barking Mad!
I WAS HOWLING HAPPILY WITH THE REST OF THE TERRIERS...
...WHEN I SAW THAT SNEAK SEÁNEEN BRANNIGAN LOOKING IN AT US.
WET!
HE LOOKED LIKE HE WAS UP TO NO GOOD (WHAT OTHER WAY DOES HE EVER LOOK?) SO I DECIDED TO KEEP AN EYE ON HIM.
DID I MENTION I AM ONE EIGHTH BLOODHOUND ON MY MOTHER'S SIDE?
EVERYBODY ELSE, THE KILMORE KILLERS INCLUDED, WAS FILING OUT ON TO THE PITCH FOR THE SECOND HALF...
TROPHY ROOM
...AND NOBODY HAD NOTICED THAT SEÁNEEN WASN'T THERE.
WET PAINT

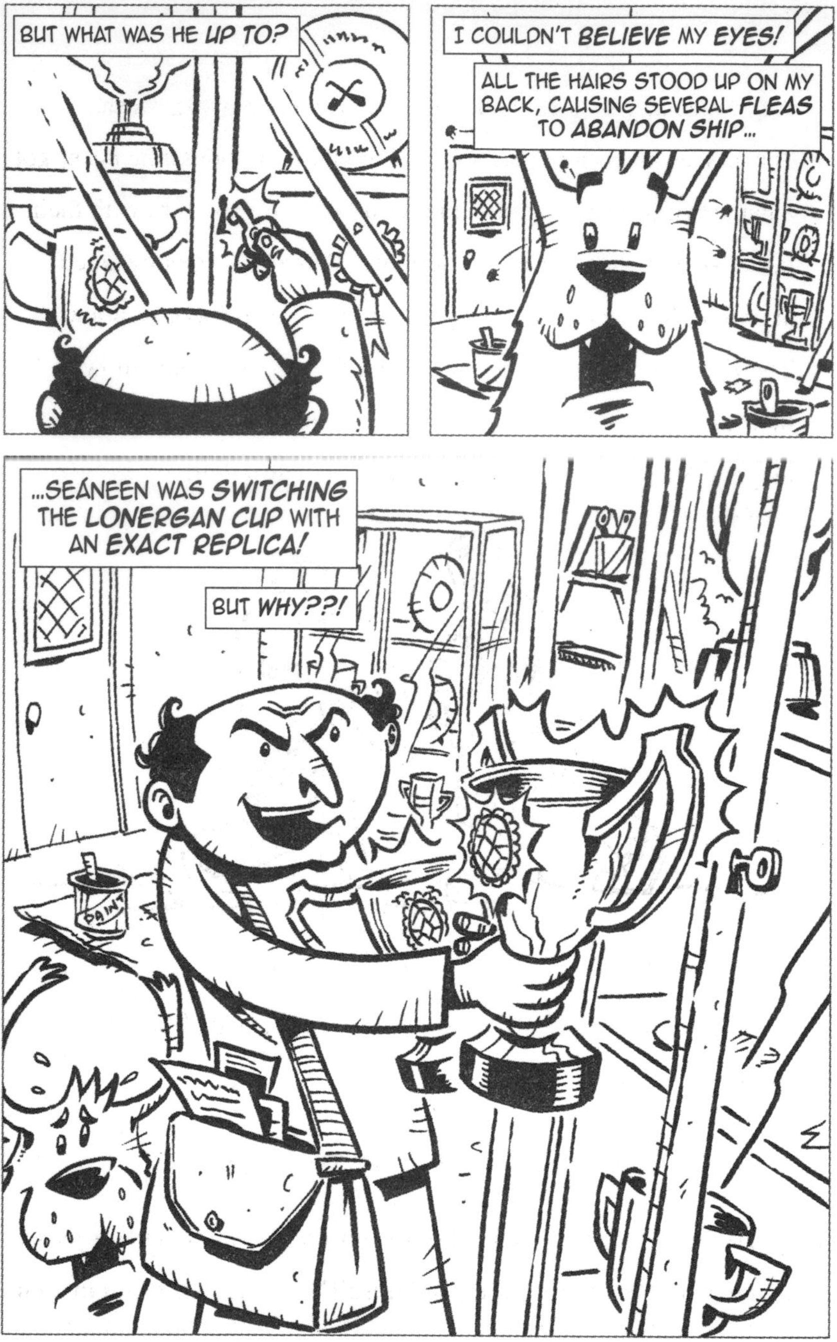
BUT WHAT WAS HE UP TO?
I COULDN'T BELIEVE MY EYES!
ALL THE HAIRS STOOD UP ON MY BACK, CAUSING SEVERAL FLEAS TO ABANDON SHIP...
...SEANEEN WAS SWITCHING THE LONERGAN CUP WITH AN EXACT REPLICA!
BUT WHY??!
PAINT

they especially took exception to Kyle Rogers playing for the Terriers, as he used to play for the Killers, even though he never got a game. They targeted him unmercifully, swiping at him with their hurls when the referee wasn't looking. Despite all the unwanted attention, Kyle managed to give them the slip and score a point! The Killers didn't like this at all and a few minutes later showed their displeasure by crushing Kyle between two of their biggest players. Kyle hit the ground and had to be carried off.

The Terriers were all furious at this grubby play. Mansize growled and fumed beside me.

'Easy, Mansize,' I said. 'Look who's coming on!'

At the side of the pitch, who was pulling on a red Terriers jersey and helmet but Fintan Lonergan himself! The Terriers stood in their positions on the pitch and clapped and whooped and hollered as he came on. A few of us even howled!

The jersey wasn't as tight a fit on him as it been when he last wore it a few months before at the *poc fada*.

He ran over to Mansize and me and said, 'Right, Rusty, I'm coming on in midfield for Kyle, he's out for the match.' He turned to Mansize. 'Don't worry, Mansize, Kyle will live. And I don't want any of us Terriers to resort to those type of bully-boy tactics either – us Terriers use our brains and our talents just as much as our brawn.'

Play resumed and Fintan quickly whispered something to Mansize and then to Liam and they both took off up the pitch towards the Kilmore goal.

As soon as Fintan got his first touch of the sliotar he hoofed it way up the pitch with a whack of almost Rory-like proportions, but way higher, the ball almost disappearing from sight it went so high. The sliotar eventually fell down towards the Kilmore goalposts, looking like it was going to be a point for the Terriers, when out of nowhere appeared Mansize and Liam Chang. Mansize lightly picked up Liam and threw him into the air, just like he was back at the highland games tossing a caber. Liam swung his hurley in mid-air and a mighty whack echoed through Carey Park as his hurley connected with the sliotar and drove it down and between the posts for a goal!

We couldn't believe our luck, we were two points ahead! The crowd couldn't believe it either and started chanting 'Terriers! Terriers!' Some of them even started howling, just like us!

Kyle peered dazedly from the sideline, a white bandage on his head.

Right from the puckout, Fintan took the advantage, gaining the ball at the Terriers' end and running up the field with the sliotar perfectly balanced on the bas of his hurley. Katie's egg-and-spoon-on-skateboard lessons had obviously done the trick! He dodged Kilmore player after Kilmore player, handpassing the ball between himself and Halfpint O'Reilly. All the Kilmore players fell back into their own half, but Fintan was too fast for them.

Just before the Kilmore goal he sidestepped Dennis Brannigan himself, who looked over to the stands for assistance from his manager, but Seáneen wasn't there. Fintan threw the sliotar high up in the air and swung his hurley, hitting the ball with a colossal crack that shook the whole of Carey Park.

The stands were still shaking with the noise of Fintan's blow to the sliotar, but they were soon shaking with the noise of cheering!

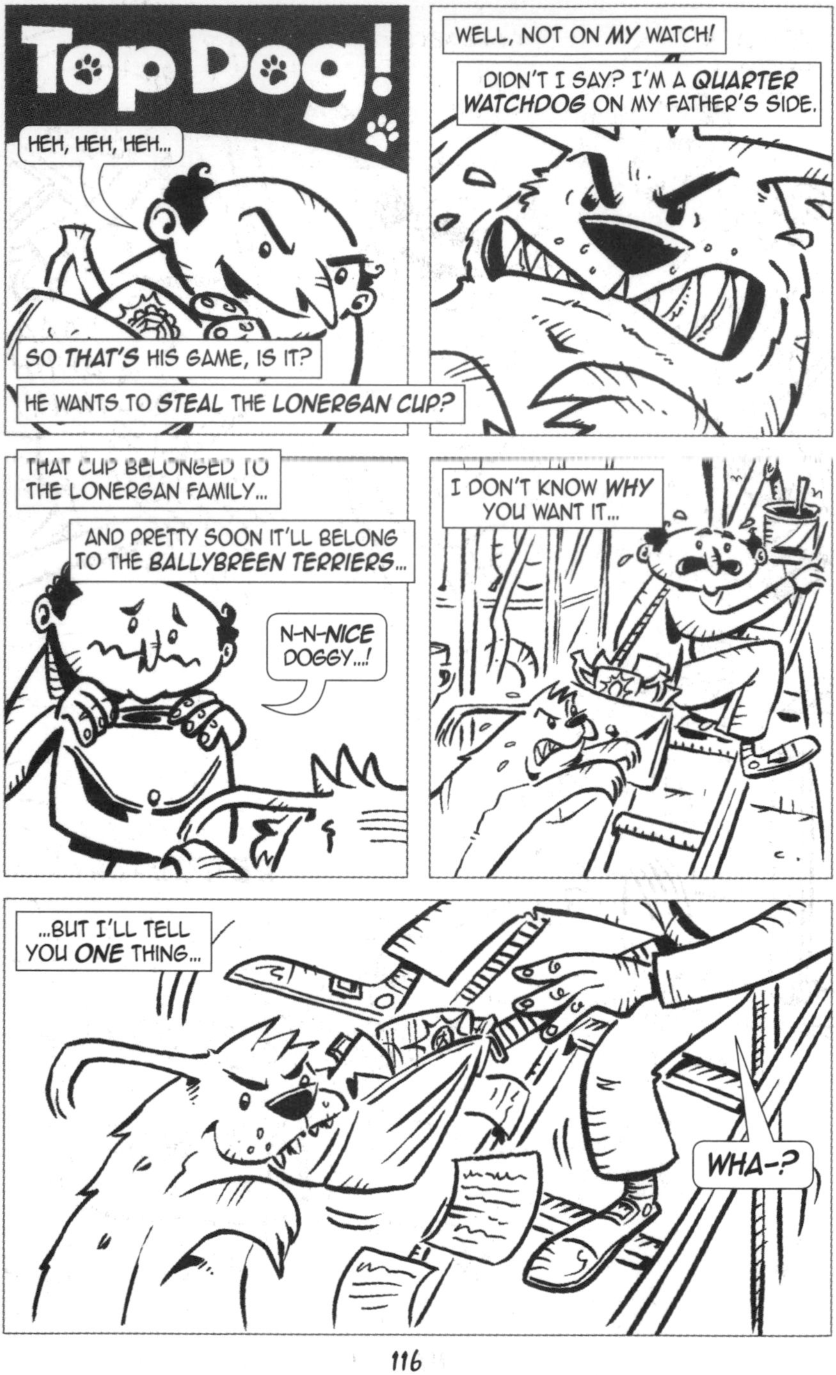
Top Dog!
HEH, HEH, HEH...
SO THAT'S HIS GAME, IS IT?
HE WANTS TO STEAL THE LONERGAN CUP?
WELL, NOT ON MY WATCH!
DIDN'T I SAY? I'M A QUARTER WATCHDOG ON MY FATHER'S SIDE.
THAT CUP BELONGED TO THE LONERGAN FAMILY...
AND PRETTY SOON IT'LL BELONG TO THE BALLYBREEN TERRIERS...
N-N-NICE DOGGY...!
I DON'T KNOW WHY YOU WANT IT...
...BUT I'LL TELL YOU ONE THING...
WHA-?

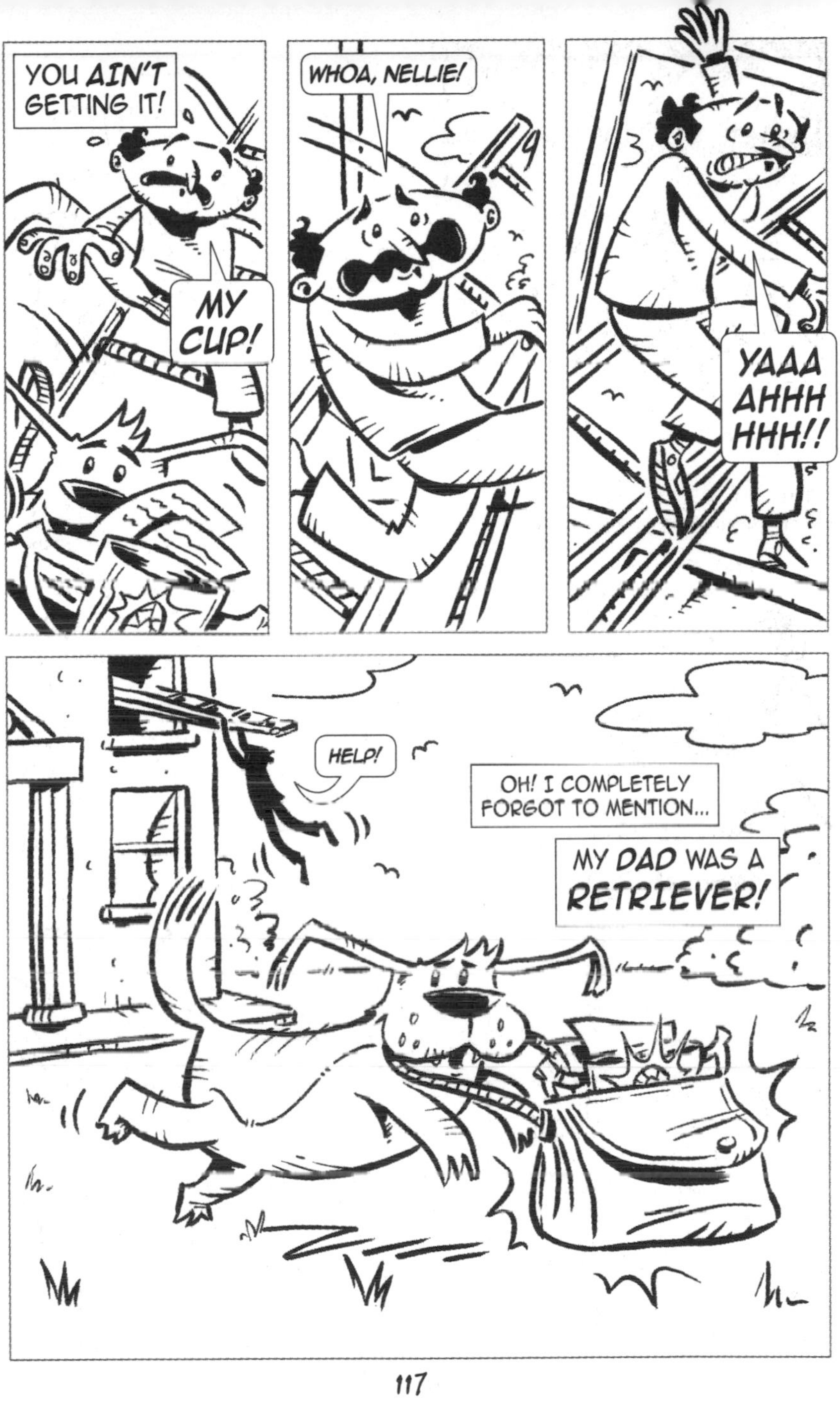
YOU AIN'T GETTING IT!
MY CUP!
WHOA, NELLIE!
YAAA AHHH HHH!!
HELP!
OH! I COMPLETELY FORGOT TO MENTION...
MY DAD WAS A RETRIEVER!

Fintan's shot was straight and true – the sliotar flew over the head of the Kilmore goalkeeper, almost parting his hair, and landed in the centre of the Kilmore goal. The green flag went up! The sound of cheering from the crowd was so deafening that we almost didn't hear the final whistle.

The Terriers had done it! We had won the Lonergan Cup! Incredibly, unbelievably, we were THE CHAMPIONS! Fintan fell to his knees on the grass, but he wasn't there for long. We crowded around him and hoisted him up on our shoulders. The cheering crowd ran onto the pitch, led by Katie 'Dinger' Bell, who threw her arms around me.

'You did it!' she screamed. 'We all did,' I shouted over the din.

Ollie appeared from nowhere and started barking his head off. He had a leather satchel in his mouth and papers were falling out of it.

'He wants to join in!' shouted Katie happily. 'No,' I said, 'something's up.' Fintan looked down from the shoulders of the Terriers' players' 'Look! He brought us the cup!' he shouted. Sure enough, the Lonergan Cup itself fell from the bag Ollie was holding, along with a bunch of papers.

I picked up one of the A4 sheets as Katie handed the cup to

Fintan. 'The Evergreen Emerald?' I read out loud. 'Never mind that now,' said Katie. Fintan held the cup high over his head. 'We've won the Lonergan Cup!' she shouted. The crowd cheered louder than ever. The Lonergan Cup was back where it belonged!

YOU'LL LAUGH, YOU'LL CRY, YOU'LL HURL.
FINTAN LONERGAN

It was the best and strangest day of my life, and it was about to get even stranger. What with the excitement of the win, and the surprise of Ollie bringing us the Cup, I quite forgot about the curious brown leather satchel bag with the papers about some sort of emerald.

It was only after the prize-giving (from which Seáneen Brannigan was mysteriously absent) when we were all on the coach home, that I noticed the bag lying on one of the seats at the front. While all the team were laughing and singing and clapping each other on the back, I opened the bag and read through the computer printouts and magazine clippings inside. I couldn't believe what I was reading. Was it true? Was the green gemstone in the Lonergan Cup really the famous long-lost Evergreen Emerald? If all these papers were right, then Fintan was going to be rolling in money!

'Fintan, you're rich!' I cried, and to the disbelieving stares of

my teammates, told them what I had learned from the papers in the leather satchel. We all goggled at the Lonergan Cup.

Fintan was quiet for a moment, then he said, 'Well, I find that story very hard to swallow. But even if it is true, if the gemstone in the Cup IS an Evergreen Emerald and IS priceless, I'm not going to keep it. I couldn't. My Grandad gave that Cup to local hurling, and that's where it's gonna stay. But you're right, Rusty, I AM rich. Rich with friends, rich with a great team and rich to be back playing a sport I love.' He smiled. 'One thing though,' he said. 'We should have a whip around and get a stronger padlock for the Carey Park trophy cabinet!'

We all laughed then and started singing, all the way back to Ballybreen, singing and howling, and howling with laughter. Ho-ho-hooooooooowwwwwwwwwllllllll!

Never give up!
Fintan
Lonergan!

Love,
Katie
Bells

Ray Rusty Arantes
Parabéns a todos!

Kyle Rogers

Rory Sweeney

iPaddy
10

HalfPint

Liam
Chang

122

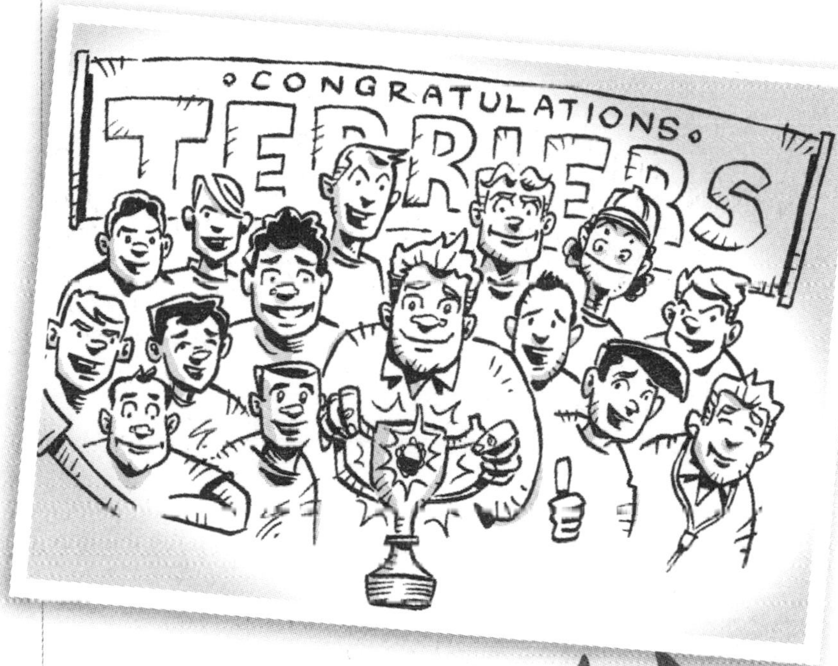
CONGRATULATIONS
TERRIERS

Phil Tutty

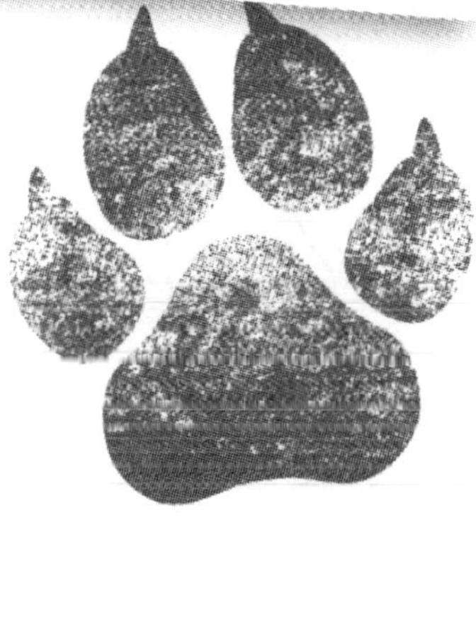

Dominic McLean

Henry Gupta

THE BIG BREAK DETECTIVES

are three friends who solve crimes – on their lunch break!
From their secret base in Lady Agatha Chesterton's School,
Danny, Kate and her brother, Little Tom, must right wrongs,
unravel mysteries, nab evil-doers and be
back in time for the end-of-break bell!

O'BRIEN

www.BigBreakDetectives.com

Alan Nolan lives and works in Bray, County Wicklow, Ireland. He is co-creator (with Ian Whelan) of *Sancho* comic which was shortlisted for two Eagle awards, and is the author and illustrator of *The Big Break Detectives Casebook* and the *'Murder Can Be Fatal'* series (The O'Brien Press).

Special thanks to Mary Webb, Michael O'Brien, Emma Byrne, Ivan O'Brien and all at The O'Brien Press.

Thanks also go out to Patricia Fitgerald at Clare County Library, Barbara and Rosena at Tallaght Library, and to David O'Connor and Tony Smyth for all their help, encouragement and support along the way.

And, finally, thanks as ever to my long-suffering family, Rachel, Adam, Matthew and Sam.

www.fintansfifteen.com

www.alannolan.ie

www.obrien.ie